Due 11/20

BESIDE STILL WATERS

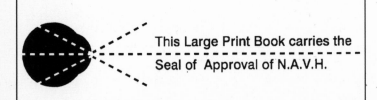

THE PSALM 23 MYSTERIES

BESIDE STILL WATERS

DEBBIE VIGUIÉ

THORNDIKE PRESS

A part of Gale, Cengage Learning

GALE
CENGAGE Learning·

Detroit • New York • San Francisco • New Haven, Conn • Waterville, Maine • London

GALE
CENGAGE Learning®

Copyright © 2012 by Debbie Viguié.
Thorndike Press, a part of Gale, Cengage Learning.

LIBRARY OF CONGRESS CATALOGING-IN-PUBLICATION DATA

Viguié, Debbie.
  Beside still waters : Psalm 23 mysteries / by Debbie Viguié. — Large Print edition.
    pages cm. — (Thorndike Press Large Print Christian Mystery)
    ISBN-13: 978-1-4104-5983-1 (hardcover)
    ISBN-10: 1-4104-5983-7 (hardcover)
    1. Murder—Investigation—Fiction. 2. Large type books. I. Title.
PS3622.I485B47 2013
813'.6—dc23   2013012940

Published in 2013 by arrangement with Debra Viguié

Printed in Mexico
1 2 3 4 5 6 7 17 16 15 14 13

This book is dedicated to all the devoted fans out there who've been waiting for so long to continue on this journey with Cindy and Jeremiah. Thank you all for caring so deeply.

Although the job of writing a book can be incredibly lonely and isolating at times, there are those who touch our lives and ease our burden. I owe a tremendous debt of gratitude to the friends, family, and colleagues who have encouraged me and helped me on this journey. Thank you for all of your efforts to keep me sane and keep me writing! Love to you all.

1

Cindy Preston loved Saturdays. She loved them even more when she was on vacation and as she finished eating breakfast at her hotel, the Waikiki Beachcomber in Honolulu, she thought that this might just be one of the best Saturdays ever. There was a stack of brochures on her table all extolling the virtues of various sights and activities on the island.

As she finished her soda she thought gratefully of Harry, the man who had originally won the trip to Hawaii at the time share sales seminar but had swapped her for the mini television she had won. A long weekend in Hawaii was just what the doctor had ordered and she'd been looking forward to it for months. She had flown in the day before and was flying out on Tuesday morning, but planned to cram as much relaxation and sight-seeing into that time as she possibly could.

She tapped the top brochure on the stack with a pink fingernail she'd had manicured for the occasion. It was Memorial Day weekend and she couldn't think of a better way to keep the holiday than by going to Pearl Harbor and seeing the Arizona Memorial.

I wonder what Jeremiah's doing? she thought as she stood and gathered her things. Jeremiah Silverman was the rabbi at the synagogue next door to the Presbyterian church where Cindy worked as a secretary. Since they had first met the previous year over the body of a dead man in the church sanctuary they had forged an unlikely alliance and a budding friendship that meant more to her than she liked to admit to herself.

He had volunteered to drop her off at the airport the day before and would be picking her up Tuesday morning when she returned.

I should have taken the whole week off work, she lamented. There was no way she was going to be in the mood for work Wednesday morning. And Geanie, her new roommate and the church's graphic designer, had made it quite clear that if she didn't come back with pictures of the wedding pavilions of a couple of the local hotels that she shouldn't come back at all. Geanie had recently become engaged to Joseph, a wealthy church member and a friend of Cindy's.

She briefly thought about changing out of her shorts into jeans before heading for the memorial, but decided against it. Looking at her overly pale legs no one would guess she was a California native. Some sun would do her good. Plus it just felt too hot to be wearing anything more than the khaki shorts and green tank top she had donned for breakfast.

As she grabbed a taxi and settled into the backseat her mind drifted back to her friends at home. She wanted to make sure to take them back some souvenirs. Although she suspected that was going to end up being boxes of chocolate covered macadamia nuts. She had nearly eaten an entire box herself last night after dinner.

"Where you from?"

Cindy jumped, startled, as she realized that the taxi driver, a large Hawaiian man who seemed to completely fill the front seat of the cab, was talking to her.

"California."

"No kidding, my cousin lives there."

"Small world," she murmured.

"How long you stay?"

"I go home Tuesday."

"Too bad."

"Yes, I wish I could stay longer," she said.

"It's a good time to see the Memorial. It's sacred ground you know."

"Because of the men who died there?" she asked.

"Because of the sacrifice, the dead, the living."

She didn't know what to say.

"You like good food?"

"Yes, do you have any recommendations?"

"Sure. You should go eat lunch at my uncle's restaurant. They have da kine plate lunch, best on island."

"Where is it?"

"It's off the base about a fifteen minute walk from where I'm dropping you off. He's great friends with the sailors. I show you and you no miss it."

"Thanks."

A few minutes later when they pulled up outside the Pearl Harbor Visitor Center he pointed out how she could find Uncle's.

"Here, I give you business card. You need taxi, you call me I take good care of you. And go to Uncle's for lunch. Tell him I sent you. He give you local discount."

"Thanks," she said. She took the business card he gave her and slipped it into her purse.

She walked into the Center and began to look around. There were displays talking about the attack on Pearl Harbor during World War II. A screen showed the few bits of footage they had of the actual attack. People were milling around quietly. She headed into the gift store and bought a small book and a couple of postcards. At the register there were miniature decks of playing cards with pictures of Hawaii on them. She added them to her purchase on an impulse.

After about an hour she boarded the boat to head on over to the U.S.S. Arizona Memorial. A tour group was on the boat as well and she listened as the guide explained what they were about to see.

"The memorial itself actually straddles the sunken Arizona. In the middle of the memorial you'll be able to look down into the water and see one of its gun turrets. The sailors who died on the Arizona are still there on the ship."

Cindy shuddered as she felt her pulse begin to race a little. She couldn't help but think about her sister who had died when they were children. Her body had been recovered, buried in a grave where family could visit. The sailors were interred in their watery grave. How hard must that have been on friends and family?

She bit her lip and forced herself to refocus on what the guide was saying. "Other ships were sunk as well. The Oklahoma capsized almost immediately. Some sailors were able to survive by escaping through the portals. The portals were so narrow, though, that only the skinniest made it out. Their friends and comrades who could not fit helped shove them through until they themselves drowned."

Horror stole through her as she thought about what those trapped men had gone through. She couldn't imagine a worse death than drowning. And yet they had had the courage to help push their friends to safety. She understood suddenly what her taxi driver had meant by sacrifice.

As they neared the dock she looked around. Leis and wreaths floated in the water all around the Memorial. *Hallowed ground,* she thought. As she stared at the floating tokens she felt tears sting her eyes.

The boat docked and a minute later she was standing on the U.S.S. Arizona Memorial and around her people's voices were hushed.

Because we're standing on top of graves, she realized as her eyes scanned the list of names on the wall which was accompanied by a plaque that proclaimed: *To the memory of the gallant men here entombed and their shipmates who gave their lives in action on December 7, 1941 on the U.S.S. Arizona.*

One older man covered in tattoos was standing, tears streaming freely down his face. She couldn't help but wonder if he'd had a relative who had been killed there or if it was just the power and poignancy of the place itself that so touched him.

She walked around, looking out at the harbor around them. She skirted the section in the middle where you could look down on the ship itself. She couldn't bring herself to look, afraid that she would start crying uncontrollably. Chills kept washing over her. The day before Pearl Harbor had just been a name to her, a place, an historical event. And now it felt so real and she mourned the men who had died there decades before she was born.

She could tell people around her were feeling the same way. A woman nearby was crying and hugging a uniformed soldier, thanking him for his service to his country. Cindy respected her reaction and felt the need to thank every member of the armed services personally and individually for their service, their sacrifice.

It was more than she'd expected to feel

and it overwhelmed her. She thought about Jeremiah. He was from Israel and like all of its citizens he had served his time in the military.

He could have been killed, just like the men here. There is so much violence in that part of the world, so many attacks though smaller than this one deadly still. And he could have lost his life in any one of them. And then I never would have met him. And I would have been killed last year.

Now she was crying freely and she had to leave. She felt like she couldn't breathe and she struggled not to think about the men who had drowned here, gasping for air when there was none.

I can breathe. There is air. In. Out.

She got onto the boat and fixed her eyes on the shore. She had been thinking of taking the boat tour around the harbor, circling Ford Island, but she couldn't. She just needed to get away.

As soon as she made it back onto dry land she hurried away from the center as fast as she could. Her mind was racing and she felt queasy. She should stop, get on one of the buses or take a taxi, but she just kept walking, sucking the warm, fragrant air into her lungs and reminding herself that she was alive.

She heard a shout and she turned and saw a man on a small boat helping a man in a wetsuit with scuba gear onto the boat. They turned and looked at her and the man on the boat waved. She gave them a little wave back before hurrying on. Everyone was so friendly in Hawaii.

That friendliness was just one thing that seemed to make the place so unique. The flower-scented air, the casual, laid-back attitude of the locals, and even the pigeon English all combined to give the place a unique feel.

She was enjoying soaking it all in so much that it even made her think of her brother who had a television travel show and was constantly visiting strange and exotic locations. Was it something akin to the sense of wonder that she had been feeling since she arrived that drove him?

Of course, Kyle always chose places that were dangerous and activities that registered somewhere between insane and suicidal. She wasn't sure if he'd been to Hawaii, but if he had he had probably found it all too safe.

Safety, though, was one thing Cindy prized highly. Hawaii was just about her speed. Anything more would make her crazy.

After walking a few more minutes Cindy made it off the base and finally found herself standing outside a little restaurant with a sign that read *Uncle's.* It made her smile. Apparently the proprietor wasn't just her cab driver's uncle, but everyone's uncle. She had heard somewhere that it was local custom to refer to older people as Auntie or Uncle and people your own age as Cousin, regardless of relation.

It was early, only just after eleven. The open sign was lit and a small hand-lettered sign declared that they opened at half past whenever and closed when they felt like it.

She laughed, beginning to feel better. The island lifestyle and slower pace was something she'd heard about, but it played out in the most interesting ways.

She pushed the door and it swung open freely. The interior was brightly lit but empty. There were half a dozen tables with chairs clustered around them. A counter at the back was positioned with a menu hanging on the wall above it.

She walked forward, perusing the menu.

She had finally settled on the Loco Moco which was supposed to be a favorite according to the sign.

Having decided she looked around for a bell to ring but saw none.

"Hello?" she called.

There was no sound from the kitchen area which she could see a sliver of through an open doorway.

"Hello?" she called, louder this time.

Silence.

Maybe they weren't open yet.

But the sign outside had been lit.

And the door had been unlocked. Maybe that wasn't uncommon here.

She turned to go and her eyes fell on an iPhone sitting on the counter. It seemed out of place. Beside it was a Tip Jar that was stuffed full.

Better just go, she told herself.

And then her eyes fell on the cash register. The drawer was open and she could see money just sitting there.

There had to be someone in the restaurant. There was no way they would just leave the drawer open and leave.

She bit her lip, torn. Finally she picked up a take-out menu and dialed the phone number listed there.

The iPhone rang and she jumped.

"You've reached Uncle. Leave me a message and tell me how you like the food."

She hung up.

There was nothing else she could do. The restaurant and the money weren't her responsibility. She walked out the door and as it swung shut she noticed an emergency contact number in the window.

It would be stupid to dial it. Obviously someone was either there or would be back soon. Maybe they were just in the bathroom.

She wanted to believe that was true, but another part of her whispered that there was something wrong. Someone could be sick or injured. Uncle must be older and he could need help.

She gritted her teeth and dialed the number. It started to ring and she heard a shrill ring coming from inside the restaurant.

And then it went to voicemail.

She hung up and took a deep breath. She glanced around. There were several other businesses close by. Maybe she should go inform someone at one of them of what she had found.

But what if someone steals the money because I didn't do everything I could? she asked herself. *And what if someone's injured and needs help?*

For all she knew Uncle was a large, overweight man who could have had a heart attack. She walked back inside and headed toward the counter.

This is stupid, it's not your job.

And she thought of the men on the Oklahoma, dying, and yet still pushing others to safety. She took a deep breath. Finding out if the owner needed help was such a little thing.

"Hello?" she shouted this time.

Still no answer.

She walked around the counter and took a step into the kitchen.

And that was when she smelled blood.

The hair on the back of her neck raised up and she gripped the doorjamb hard.

Uncle could have fallen, hit his head.

She forced herself to take another step, and then another.

And then she could see all of the kitchen. She saw white countertops, stainless appliances, and a dead man on the floor lying in a pool of blood, a bullet hole in his forehead.

2

Cindy screamed and then clamped a hand over her mouth as she realized that whoever killed the man might still be nearby.

She dialed 911 with shaking fingers and when the dispatcher came on she explained where she was and what had happened in a halting, terrified whisper.

And the woman made her repeat the information several times until she could hear sirens in the distance.

"They're almost here," she whispered and hung up.

A minute later two uniformed officers came through the front door, hands on their guns.

"He's over here," she called, voice shaking.

The one officer pushed past her and the second took her elbow and steered her back out to the dining room and had her sit at one of the tables. She put her small bag of purchases from the Pearl Harbor store on the table and after a minute opened up the deck of cards and began to shuffle them in her hands.

When the officer came back to her he raised an eyebrow.

"Nervous habit, sorry," she muttered. The deck had been held together with just plastic and there was no case so instead of dumping the cards back in the bag she slipped the deck into her pocket.

"Ma'am, I'm Officer George Li. What happened here?" the officer as ked, staring at her intently.

She closed her eyes for just a moment, wishing that none of this had ever happened. Or wishing that instead it had happened back home and she was talking to Detective Mark Walters. Wishing couldn't change anything though so she took a deep breath and told him everything she knew.

It's good to be a rabbi, Jeremiah reflected to himself as he greeted people after the Shabbat service. The sun was shining brightly outside and children's laughter drifted into the building. Everyone was in a good mood and telling him how helpful they'd found his comments on the day's Torah reading.

It was nice when it was like this. Some

days just seemed made for happiness. The only thing that would have made it better would have been the promise of a late night meal with Cindy. He was glad she had finally taken the trip to Hawaii, though. If anyone needed, deserved, a vacation it was her.

"Rabbi," a wizened old man said, grasping his hand with shaking fingers. "It is good I came here today."

"We are pleased you made your way to us."

"I think, I think you are the person I need to talk to."

"I'd be happy to listen to whatever it is you wish to speak about."

The old man looked around, bright eyes furtive. "Not now. Not here."

"I am available weekdays in my office," Jeremiah said.

The old man nodded quickly. "Good, *ja. Danke.* I will come on Wednesday."

"If you have a card I can have my secretary call you to set a time," Jeremiah suggested.

The old man shook his head fiercely. "*Das glaube ich nicht. Nein.* I will come Wednesday morning and then . . . then we have much to discuss."

The old man shook his head and then turned and walked away.

Jeremiah couldn't help but stare after him. He had never seen the man before but it was not uncommon for visitors to the area to attend services in the synagogue. Something about the man's demeanor troubled him, though, even more than the fact that he was speaking German.

"Who was that?" Marie, Jeremiah's secretary asked as she walked up beside him.

"Apparently someone who wants to speak with me. He'll be coming by the office Wednesday morning."

"Did you get his name?" she asked, voice laced with suspicion.

He smiled at her. "No, but do not worry, Marie. I'm sure such an old man is harmless."

His words seemingly placated her but they did nothing to calm his own mind. He turned aside to greet a young couple and did his best to put it from his thoughts.

Whatever the old man had to say would have to wait until Wednesday. Just like dinner with Cindy would have to wait until Tuesday.

Three hours later Cindy felt like she was going to drop from exhaustion. She'd answered all of Officer Li's questions at least four times. Then she'd had to go through it all over again with Detective Robinson when he arrived. She was beginning to feel that one of the worst things about being a witness was being made to feel like a suspect when the police questioned you like they did.

"I think that about does it," Detective Robinson said at last, snapping shut his notebook.

"I'd like to go back to my hotel now," she said.

"Sure, I'll take you," he said, moving to stand up.

Standing next to him she was overwhelmed by his height. He had to be nearly seven feet tall. She craned her neck to look up at him. He was deeply tanned and wore his black hair a little longer than she was used to seeing.

He led her outside and she got into his car and rested her head against the seat. A minute later they pulled away from the restaurant and she couldn't help but breathe a sigh of relief.

"You haven't exactly been welcomed with the spirit of aloha," he said.

"Things were going really well," she said, trying to keep the exhaustion and misery out of her voice. Why was it that death seemed to follow her everywhere she went?

"Well, at least you'll have an interesting story to tell your grandkids someday."

"I have enough of those to last a lifetime."

"That sounds intriguing. Care to share?"

"No. All I want is to get back to my hotel, grab my bathing suit and hit the beach."

He grinned.

"What?"

"Spoken like a tourist."

"What, you can't tell me locals don't go to the beach?"

He laughed. "Of course we do, but we're usually already wearing our swimming suits under our clothes."

"You're joking."

"No, ma'am."

"I wish I had more time here," she said.

"You need a local to show you around."

"I don't know. I think I might have seen enough local color."

"Dumb luck. But let me make it up to you. Would you like to have dinner with me tomorrow night?" he asked.

"Excuse me?" she asked, sure she had misheard him.

"Dinner. I'm asking you out," he said with a slow smile it was impossible not to be charmed by.

"Oh, well, I don't think —"

"I get it. You've got a guy back home waiting for you, right?"

She felt the heat rise to her cheeks. "Well, no, not exactly." She sighed in frustration. It wasn't like she and Jeremiah were dating. They were just friends. Why then did his face come instantly to mind when the detective asked her out?

"So, it's complicated, but there really isn't a good reason why you can't have dinner with me."

"Yes," she blurted out. "How did you get that from what I said?"

"Detective. Turns out it's a skill that helps in all areas of life. So, if there's no good reason, then we'll go out to dinner tomorrow night, talk story, have a good time."

"That doesn't sound like a question," she accused.

"It's not. But here's one: what time do you eat dinner?"

"Six-thirty."

"Good answer."

When he pulled into the parking garage beneath her hotel it was almost too soon. She opened her door. "Well, thank you, Detective."

"Please, call me Kapono."

"Alright. It was a pleasure meeting you, Kapono."

"I will see you tomorrow night."

26

Something in the way he said it made her blush and she exited the car quickly. She walked to the escalator that would lead upstairs to the lobby of the hotel. She turned and gave a wave as he drove on.

Her stomach rumbled noisily, reminding her that she still hadn't had lunch. On a whim she turned away from the escalator and walked a few steps until she reached the sidewalk. The hotel was next door to the International Marketplace which was brimming with stores and stalls selling every Hawaiian trinket imaginable and then some.

She walked through, doing her best to ignore the man who tried to get her to pick an oyster to get a pearl and the brightly colored sarongs that beckoned from racks with large discount signs. She saw a sign for the food court and she kept walking, deeper into the Marketplace until she finally found what she was looking for.

The first food stand was Rainbow Sushi. It was the tiniest little structure imaginable, no bigger than the shed in her parents' yard back home. The menu covered the entire front of the stand and she gawked at the variety of sushi available. More amazing still was how affordable it was.

She hesitated for only a moment before ordering a California roll, tuna tamaki, and a lava roll. She watched in awe as the woman behind the counter prepared it all with swift hands. Less than five minutes later her sushi was ready and she took it to one of the metal tables to eat.

The table next to her had a couple of locals, older women, who looked like they were finishing up their own lunches.

"Shot in own kitchen. Terrible," she heard one woman say.

Cindy froze, chopsticks in hand. It had only been a few hours, surely they couldn't be talking about Uncle. Word couldn't have spread that quickly.

"Yeah, but Uncle mixed up with bad types. He get what coming to him."

Then again, maybe news traveled faster here.

The first speaker nodded. "Someone should have kicked him in the okole years ago."

The other one nodded and then they got up to toss their trash. Cindy struggled with her own curiosity and couldn't believe that she wanted to stop the women and ask them about Uncle.

What's wrong with me, she wondered. *This has nothing to do with me. I go home in a couple of days and I can forget I ever even heard about Uncle.*

But there was another part of her that knew she'd never be able to forget him lying there in a pool of blood with the bullet hole in his forehead. And she worried that she'd never be able to have peace about it until she knew that his killer had been caught. *A reason to stay in touch with Kapono.*

She picked up a piece of lava roll and popped it in her mouth. The flavors exploded and she closed her eyes to better savor the taste. Twenty minutes later when she finished eating she had to admit it was the best sushi she'd ever had in her life. It was almost good enough to make her forget her morning. Almost, but not quite.

Finished she took her time walking back through the Marketplace, trying to decide what gifts to take home. No matter how hard she tried to focus her thoughts elsewhere, though, they kept returning to the body she had seen that morning.

Whoever had killed him had left the money in the cash register and the tip jar. That meant it wasn't some kind of robbery. *Unless they panicked and ran,* she thought. She hadn't seen anyone leaving the building when she walked up to it so it seemed unlikely that her arrival had scared the killer off.

At last, disgusted with her ability to focus

on anything else, she headed back to her hotel. Once in the lobby she made her way to the concierge desk and took a seat. Ten minutes later she was back in her room, satisfied that the luau she would be heading to shortly and the sightseeing cruise she'd booked for the next morning would help her take her mind off of everything that had happened.

In the meantime the ocean was calling so she changed into her bathing suit, threw on a cover-up, grabbed her towel and headed for the beach.

She had to walk along the street, passing a myriad of shops aimed at tourists to get to the beach. Waikiki beach was a comparatively small strip of sand separated from the main road by a low wall. Still it drew crushes of people to it and now she was one of them.

As she passed by an electronics store something caught her eye and she stopped. There, on a television screen in the window, was a news report about the murder of Uncle. They flashed his face up on the screen and she stared at it transfixed. Next they supplanted his picture with a blank outline of a head and a question mark over it. The message was clear — the killer was unknown. She stared intently at that dark outline.

"Who are you?" she whispered.

Mark was hunched over the keyboard of his computer in his home office, scrolling through page after page of information. While he was still suspended from active duty on the police force he had been doing what he could to find out on his own exactly who his late partner was.

Paul Dryer, that was the name he had known his partner under. Apparently, though, that was a lie. The body of the real Paul Dryer had been recovered from the mass grave at the Green Pastures campsite a couple of months before. The real Paul Dryer had been kidnapped as a child by a dangerous cult and apparently killed.

No one knew yet who the man who had been his partner, who had been masquerading as Paul Dryer, really was. He had tried reaching out to Paul's family, but couldn't get them to return his calls. He wondered who at the department had been assigned the case and whether or not they were having any more luck.

He heard the front door open and a few moments later Buster jumped into his lap.

Mark rubbed the beagle behind the ears.

The last several months had been terrible ones for him and his wife, Traci. The dog represented the one bright spot in all of that and the more time he was forced to spend at home the more attached he became.

"We're back from our walk," his wife, Traci, said as she entered the room.

"So I see."

She kissed his cheek. "How's it going?"

"It's not," he said with a sigh. He leaned back in his chair. "I've tried searching for other kids that went missing around the same time who were roughly the same age."

"You think NP knew he wasn't the Dryer's lost son?"

NP stood for Not Paul. It was what they had taken to calling him for ease of communication. Somehow it seemed better than calling him John Doe even though that was essentially what he was.

"Your guess is as good as mine. For all we know he thought he was the real Paul Dryer."

"I can't even imagine what the family must be going through right now. I know if I were them I'd be in total denial. I mean, think about it. As far as they're concerned they lost Paul and NP all on the same day."

It had to be unimaginable.

Traci touched his shoulder. "Do you have

an appointment with the psychologist to-day?"

He shook his head. "I'm going to find someone else to talk to. That guy gives me the creeps."

"Are you sure?" she asked.

He could hear the concern in her voice. She was right to feel that way. If he was ever going to be allowed back on the force it was only going to happen after the mandatory hours of counseling they had assigned him. He knew that and knew he had to suck it up and get it done even though he didn't want to talk to anyone about what had happened in that interrogation room two months earlier.

Why did you put me in this position, NP?

"Yes. I know it's important. I just need to find someone else to talk to."

"If there's anything I can do to help, just let me know," she said.

"You help just by being here," he said.

She kissed him again and then left the room.

Traci was his angel. He didn't deserve her, but he'd needed her more than he ever had before. She had held him when he cried for his dead partner. She had woken him from the nightmares that plagued him after he had tortured the suspect in his custody. She had listened while he babbled on about finding out the truth about both Paul Dryers.

Somehow he would make it all up to her. He had to.

He glanced up at a picture on the wall. It was him and Paul the day they had been partnered up together. "Who are you?" he whispered.

When Jeremiah finally made it home Captain, his German Shepherd, was waiting eagerly at the door for him, his leash in his mouth.

Jeremiah couldn't help but laugh at the sight. "Okay, boy, I get the hint. Let me just change real quick."

Ten minutes later, wearing jeans and a polo shirt Jeremiah walked Captain down the sidewalk. He could feel the dog's contentment and he had to admit that he'd grown to enjoy their walks nearly as much.

The dog's previous owner had taken him for walks in the park, but Captain was happy enough just strolling around the neighborhood. And since Jeremiah still wasn't sure if friends or enemies of the dog's former master might be looking for Captain, Jeremiah much preferred to walk someplace a little more secluded, less public.

He was probably being paranoid. It had been six months since Captain's old owner had ended up dead on Jeremiah's front lawn. Fortunately the police had assumed that the man was another victim of the group killing the homeless and stealing dogs. When the guilty had been brought to justice the file on the man calling himself Peter Wallace had been closed. At least as far as the police were concerned.

As far as Jeremiah was concerned the murder of Peter Wallace remained unsolved. Worse, it was clear to the rabbi that Wallace had been coming to his house in the middle of the night when he was shot less than a block away.

Why was Wallace coming to see him? He knew they'd recognized each other in the park but he had desperately hoped the other would leave him alone. It was even more disturbing to think about the fact that his killer was on the loose and had been so close to Jeremiah's home. Had he known where Wallace was heading? If so, when would he put in an appearance at Jeremiah's doorstep?

He didn't like any of it. Six months had passed but he still felt on edge all the time, afraid that his fragile web of lies was soon going to be put to the test and would unravel before his very eyes. Not only would that be a personal tragedy but it would also throw the synagogue into chaos, destroying it spiritually if not physically.

Not to mention what knowing the truth would do to Cindy, he thought. He sighed. Lately it seemed like she was seldom far from his thoughts. There was no help for it and he'd given up trying to fight it.

Captain followed him as he turned down a tree lined street. He couldn't help but feel like the dog was part of the bigger mystery in a way he hadn't yet guessed. He didn't like waiting for something to happen. Every nerve, every instinct screamed at him to *do* something.

But until a threat presented itself there was nothing to do.

You could leave. Go somewhere else completely, start over.

Appealing as the idea was, he had to admit he didn't want to. In his gut he knew that had more to do with Cindy than it did with the members of the synagogue, even though he cared for them a great deal. It wouldn't be the first time he had to leave others behind to wonder what had happened to him.

A few blocks later they turned again and Jeremiah tried to focus on the trees and the birds around him. He breathed in deeply of the fresh air. He loved California. It would be a hard place to leave.

Another turn brought them back onto his street. A few steps later he felt himself slowing and he looked down. A moment later he came to a stop at the exact spot that Wallace had been shot before staggering down the street to die on his lawn.

He turned a slow circle, looking at the houses, the trees, the cars, everything. He had done so a dozen times before but he tried to imagine where the shooter would have been. The shot had been fired from only a few feet distant and the gun must have had a silencer since no one had heard a thing.

Captain whined deep in his throat, anxious to get home. Although Jeremiah sometimes wondered if the dog knew what had happened to his owner here and hated the place. As he had a hundred times before Jeremiah tried to picture the killer in his mind.

"Who are you?" he whispered.

3

Dissatisfied with the crush of people at Waikiki Cindy headed back to her hotel. The concierge had told her that the hotel on the north shore where her luau was that evening had miles of sandy beaches. She grabbed her clothes for the luau and grabbed a taxi, hoping to get in some better beach time before the luau started. She even told herself that she'd be helping Geanie by scoping out the resort as a possible wedding location.

The taxi driver seemed less inclined to conversation than her previous one and kept the radio on. Cindy sat back in the seat and stared out at the beautiful scenery including sweeping mountains and majestic ocean. Snatches of music and news caught her attention, but she tried to focus on the beauty around her.

"The reefing of the historic navy vessel is set to take place in just a few days. In other news there's more trouble for the proposed building site of the new megaresort on the north shore of the island. Archaeologists have discovered yet another mass grave site. All development has been halted while a full assessment of the area can be conducted. This might prove the final nail in the coffin to a project that had been estimated to bring in nearly one hundred million in revenue and create hundreds of new jobs."

The driver chuckled deep in his throat.

"What's so funny?" she asked.

"These companies come here with no respect for the culture, the island, and this time the ancestors have had enough."

Cindy wasn't quite sure how to respond to him and decided it was best if she didn't. It sounded like this might be a political hot topic and she should steer clear.

The newscaster went on. "— garnered mixed reactions from locals." A selection of sound bites followed.

"We need this revenue for the local economy," a woman said.

"The tourists have Waikiki. Why they need come up here? The north shore should be for kama'aina."

She could see her driver nodding his head and she slunk down further into her seat.

When he finally dropped her at the front of the hotel where the luau would be it wasn't a minute too soon. As soon as she stepped into the hotel's lobby she felt herself begin to relax. It was open and inviting and smelled heavenly from all the flowers growing about.

She made her way through the lobby and outside to the pool area. Beyond it the ocean beckoned and she went. Beaches in the state were all completely public so she didn't feel the least bad as she spread out her beach towel she'd brought with her and sat herself down on it.

There were only about a dozen other people on the beach, far fewer than were gathered around the elaborate pool several yards behind her. Most were tourists like her, but there were a couple that looked more like locals. Cindy tucked her knees up under her chin and hugged herself as she stared at the ocean and breathed in deeply of the salt air. This was what she always thought of when she thought of Hawaii. She was thrilled that it more than lived up to her expectations.

She closed her eyes and felt the sun shining down on her, warming her within and without. Slowly she felt her muscles begin to relax one by one until only her mind was tense. Try as she might she couldn't get the murder out of her head. She couldn't help but wonder what Jeremiah would say about it.

She knew exactly what Detective Mark would say. It was none of her business and she should stay clear of it. Only she was the one who had found the body. In a way didn't that sort of make it her business?

She sighed and stretched out on the blanket, securing a pair of sunglasses over her eyes. She thought again about Jeremiah and wished he was there to share the gorgeous view and to talk with. She enjoyed the conversations she'd been having with him more than any others she could ever recall.

Over the last couple of months they had talked about so much, religion, work, science, art, her family. But never his family. It was odd. He had heard a hundred stories from her childhood and she couldn't think of a single one from his that he had shared. No stories, in fact, that dealt with his life before coming to live in Pine Springs, California.

She didn't know why, but hoped that someday he would open up more. Of course, she wasn't entirely blameless. After all, she'd never told him her most important story of all, the one about her sister and how she died. Cindy winced at the very thought and then jerked a minute later when she felt water hit her toes.

She sat up quickly. The tide was coming in. She quickly dragged her blanket and bag to higher ground and then sat back down.

It had gotten dark quickly and she glanced up and saw rainclouds overhead. She felt a splat on her nose followed by another on her arm. Then the sky seemed to open up and rain poured down. Several of the beach-goers made a beeline back to the hotel. The couple that she suspected were local didn't seem to mind though. They were walking down the beach, talking and holding hands.

They came up close to her and the guy flashed her a smile which she returned.

"You no go inside with the others?" he asked.

She shrugged. "I'm already wearing a swimsuit."

The girl smiled. "We have a saying in the islands. You no like the weather, wait five minutes."

It made Cindy laugh. The couple gave her a final smile and then continued strolling down the beach. They were right, too. After about five minutes the rain eased up and shortly afterward stopped completely. About ten minutes after that many of those who had sought shelter returned.

Cindy checked her watch. She still had about an hour before the luau was scheduled to begin. She decided that the local couple had the right idea. She stuffed her towel inside her bag, slung the bag over her shoulder, and began walking down the beach.

As she walked she picked up a couple of interesting bits of seashell and deposited them in her bag. A light breeze sprang up and it whipped her hair into her face. The sun was beginning to sink toward the horizon and she realized it was probably time to turn back.

She rounded a small bend in the beach and stopped short as she saw a vast expanse of ground that looked like it had been partially cleared of trees and grass. A few heaping mounds of dirt were scattered around, like some giant dog had been digging in the earth for a prized bone.

She stared for a moment and then heard the sudden, sharp sounds of arguing. Startled she swiveled her head and saw two men pulling a kayak up on the beach. They picked something up out of it that was wrapped in a tarp and they began moving toward one of the holes.

The hair prickled on the back of her neck as she clearly heard one of the men say, "Don't drop him. The bones need to be intact."

"I didn't drop her so why you complaining?" the second man asked.

This had to be the burial site and the location for the planned resort she'd heard about on the radio.

A third man appeared from behind one of the mounds. He turned and saw her, the sun glinting off his dark hair. He raised his hand as though to shield his eyes and she waved, not wanting to disturb them. Then she turned and beat a hasty retreat, sure that she'd seen enough bodies for one day, even if these were old skeletons.

By the time she made it back to the resort the sun had set. She used the bathroom near the pool to change into her clothes for the luau. Then she joined a long line of people waiting to get in.

Long tables were set and waiting and she could see buffet tables loaded with food. The scents were delicious and they made her mouth water even as she found a place at one of the tables. She was soon joined by a couple about her age. The woman had long dark blonde hair and the man had wavy black hair. They introduced themselves as Jean and Charles. She soon discovered that the couple lived on one of the other islands and was on vacation. She was also fascinated to learn that he was an archaeologist.

"Have you heard about what's going on with the resort they want to build down the beach?" Cindy asked as they waited for their table to be excused to get in the buffet line.

"Hard not to," Charles said with a shake of his head. "It's difficult on everyone when something like this happens."

"Is it normal to find mass grave sites like that?" she asked, unable to control her curiosity, particularly since having just observed the site.

"Sure. A couple of years ago a group of sixty bodies was discovered in one area of our island. Think of them as the equivalent of modern graveyards. Plus, the historic population was not that much different than the current one. Whether you live in the sixteenth century or the twenty-first century you still want to be as close to the ocean as possible. That makes it challenging here in the islands because the current population sits right on top of the bones of the ancient population."

She shuddered. "That's a little gruesome . . . a little too Poltergeist."

Jean chuckled as she took a sip of her punch.

George continued. "Most of the companies who do archaeology in the islands specialize in conservation resource management. There are a lot of laws on the books about how remains are to be treated when they are found. Someone wants to put in a new septic tank and a body is found usually we can have it reinterred with a blessing a short distance away and mark the spot so that anyone who wants to can visit it. When you start dealing with multiple bodies, though, the most desirable solution is to leave them where they're at."

"Even if that means the hotel can't be built?" Cindy asked.

"Exactly," Jean chimed in.

She thought of what she'd heard on the radio. Clearly the islanders had mixed thoughts about whether that was a good thing or a bad thing.

Their table was finally called and soon Cindy was feasting on roast pig, teriyaki beef, and lomi lomi salmon. She couldn't remember food ever tasting so delicious and Jean and Charles had so many funny stories about living in the islands that it kept her laughing all through dinner.

The show portion of the evening was

spectacular and she marveled at the dancers, particularly the fire knife dancer who closed out the show. When it was all over the last thing she wanted was to leave, but after saying goodnight to Jean and Charles she got another taxi to return her to her hotel.

This taxi driver was talkative, but mostly he went on about his daughter who had been one of the featured dancers in the show. Cindy was pleased to be able to tell him how much she had enjoyed her performance and the man's enthusiasm and pride were infectious.

When he finally dropped her off at her hotel she made her way slowly back to her room. It was moments like this she really missed having someone to discuss the evening with and her thoughts once again turned to Jeremiah. It would be well after midnight back home, though, so she didn't call.

After showering, Cindy changed into her pajamas and then turned on the television, hoping to find something to watch that would help her unwind. She stopped when she recognized the dining room of Uncle's restaurant.

A reporter was standing in front of the restaurant while the camera focused over his left shoulder to the interior where a couple of police officers could be seen.

Change the channel, she told herself.

Instead she turned up the volume.

". . . was the grizzly site of a murder today. Makana Onakea was found dead today in the kitchen of his restaurant. Police have confirmed that he had been shot. It's unclear at this time what might have motivated the attack and police aren't saying if they have any suspects. We have learned that it was a tourist who discovered his body earlier today."

Cindy felt her stomach tighten. *No, leave me out of it,* she begged silently.

"Onakea, who was simply known as Uncle to restaurant patrons, was 56. He opened the restaurant twenty years ago and has been serving local favorites since then. We'll keep you updated as we get more information about this senseless crime."

Cindy turned the television off and tucked her knees up under her chin. She again fought down a sudden urge to call Jeremiah. He would be picking her up at the airport on Tuesday and she could tell him all about it then.

She grabbed the deck of cards she'd bought at the gift shop and sat down at the table in the room to play some solitaire. She just hoped it would help her calm down enough to get to sleep.

Sunday morning dawned and Cindy was standing on a dock, watching the sun dance over the water. The sight moved her, stirred her spiritually. It was impossible not to feel somehow closer to God there in that place. She was a few minutes early and she savored the moments spending time in prayer and contemplation.

A couple minutes later the rest of the tourists arrived and the crew began to help them aboard. There were twenty of them going out. The boat tour circled part of the island and then they would stop in one spot where they could go snorkeling on a reef for an hour. She didn't plan to get in the water but she was fully prepared to enjoy the sights and the sounds of being out on it.

Cindy stepped up to the boat, a beautiful white catamaran called *Pearl of the Sea.* One of the crew offered her his hand to steady her as she stepped on board. She looked at him and realized in surprise that she recognized him as one of the men she had seen at the archaeological site the night before.

"Oh! Hello again," she said, feeling awkward as she simultaneously smiled at him and tripped.

His grin changed quickly to a frown. He searched her face, clearly trying to figure out how they knew each other. "Careful, it will take a minute to get your sea legs," he said.

"Sorry," she said, grabbing onto a rail and letting go of his hand.

She felt like an idiot.

She moved to take a seat. The boat was rocking gently and she found that it was indeed going to take her a minute to feel stable on the boat. Some passengers stood at the rails, others were seated in chairs on deck.

Cindy made her way to one of the chairs and sat gratefully. She glanced around at the other passengers, mostly couples and at least one family of five. Everyone was smiling and laughing, soaking up the sun, happy and carefree.

She envied them with a sudden, intense rush of feeling. What would it be like to be them? Her own life often felt so small and stifled. The truth was her sister's death when they were children had affected her deeply. It had thrown a pall over her entire life, she realized with painful clarity.

She had tried to live such a life of safety, tried to control everything and ended up being just scared and secretly miserable. Maybe that was one of the reasons she had always felt such anger toward her brother, Kyle. He traveled the world doing reckless stunts for his television travel show. She'd always thought he was needlessly risking his life and she had nearly hated him for it. Now, sitting on the catamaran under the Hawaiian sun, surrounded by ocean, she realized that he had been *living*.

She was the one who had been dying.

And then she thought of Jeremiah. The murderous events she had gotten involved with the last year had strengthened her, helped her put aside much of her fear. Though he hadn't caused that, he'd only been the person there by her side going through it with her, she was still grateful to him. She credited him with helping her change, even if the change was slow.

As she thought of him she wondered if he could help her grow so much more, step out into the world with boldness and courage. She couldn't help but feel that with him by her side she could do anything.

"Aloha! Welcome aboard, everyone."

She turned to look at the speaker. He was the man who had helped her onto the boat.

"My name is Al. On behalf of the crew of the *Pearl of the Sea* I'd like to welcome you onboard. Sodas and water are in the coolers. The restroom is downstairs. If there's anything we can do to make your experience today more enjoyable just let us know. We'll be getting underway here in just a minute. So, sit back and relax."

A minute later she felt the boat begin to turn and then they were headed out to sea. After a minute they picked up speed until it felt like the boat was practically jumping the waves.

Cindy breathed in deep of the fresh, salty air as her stomach lurched with the boat. She saw some of her fellow passengers pointing to the bow of the ship and she gathered from the snatches of conversation she heard that someone had spotted dolphins.

As interested as she was in seeing them she was more interested in trying to regain her equilibrium. Finally the boat turned again and slowed slightly and the motion became gentler. Now they were cruising, nearly parallel to the shore and she marveled at the scenery. Green mountains devoid of human life beckoned. It was such a contrast to busy Honolulu and yet it was such a short distance away from the city.

Maybe that was part of the magic of Hawaii. Most of it was still wild, untamed.

Spend enough time there, step past the boundaries of Waikiki, and the veneer of civilization began to fall away and primitive tropic wilderness beckoned.

"It's like a Siren song."

She glanced up, startled. Al was standing, staring from the mountains to the ocean and then finally looking at her.

"Yes. It's so . . ."

"Wild?" he asked with a smile.

She nodded. "That's the word that came to mind."

"You know there are places in the islands where no man has set foot?"

"That's fantastic," she murmured. It was also a little frightening in some ways. She had spent her life living in urban areas, and while she had been to places like Yosemite even that seemed knowable, controllable.

"I'm sorry, I didn't mean to be rude earlier," he said. "I'm just trying to remember where I know you from."

"Oh, nowhere really. I saw you last night on the north shore at the place where they've found those bodies, and it just surprised me to see you again. I assumed you were an archaeologist."

He gave her a tight smile. "It's a small island. Most of us work more than one job and we do what's needed to help out when there is a need."

"Oh, that makes sense," she said, feeling both embarrassed and intensely grateful that she only had one job to contend with back home.

"Well, nice to officially meet you. I'm Al."

"Cindy," she said quickly.

"You staying here long, Cindy?" he asked.

"Just a couple more days."

"That's the problem with being a tourist. The time flies so quickly."

"Yes, it does."

"Well, once you get in that water time will completely fall away from you. You'll forget all about it. It's just you and the fishes of the deep."

"It sounds nice, but I'm not going in the water."

"You can't miss it. It's an amazing experience," he said with a frown.

"I believe you, I just can't."

Before he could say anything one of the other crewmembers shouted out for him.

Al waved at the guy. "Gotta go. Nice talking."

"You, too," she said, staring for a moment as he walked across the ship, not a hint of unsteadiness in his stride.

She turned her eyes to the ocean. It was beautiful, magnificent. In the distance she swore she saw a fin break the surface and she sucked in her breath. It was also deadly.

Nearly an hour after leaving the dock, the catamaran was anchored in clear blue waters and one by one the passengers were taking turns stepping off the back of the ship and into the water. Cindy, though, was happily stretched out in her deck chair enjoying the sun. She had her back to the snorkelers and sat facing the open ocean.

"Mind if I sit with you?"

Cindy looked up to see a jovial looking middle aged woman smiling down at her.

"Be my guest," Cindy said, waving to the chair beside her.

"Thanks, I'm Marge, by the way," the woman said, sitting heavily down.

"Cindy. Pleased to meet you."

"This is my idea of vacationing. Looking at the ocean, soaking up the sun. It would be perfect if I hadn't let my husband convince me to leave my book back in the hotel room. I'm surprised a young thing like you isn't out in that water seeing all there is to see," Marge said.

"I don't swim," Cindy said.

"Oh, that's a shame. I'm not very good at it myself otherwise I'd be out there with my husband," Marge said, sounding a bit wistful.

Once upon a time Cindy had been very good at swimming but that was when she was little. Back when her sister was still alive. She shook her head, not wanting to introduce her own dark clouds into an otherwise beautiful day.

"What book are you reading?" she asked to get both her and Marge off the topic.

"Oh, this fascinating book about local legends and crimes. This man who used to work for the police now writes books about the local stories in several regions of the country. Gerald Wilson is his name. I just love all of his books. He's going to have a new one coming out soon about southern California."

"So I'd heard," Cindy said, trying to keep her voice neutral.

"Oh, you've heard of him!" Marge said, sounding delighted.

Cindy nodded. Not only had she heard of him, she had been interviewed by him for his book on southern California regarding the Passion Week Killer. That was definitely something she didn't want to get into with Marge.

She wanted a quiet vacation, free from serial killers, thieves, and murderers.

Too late, she thought, suppressing a sigh.

"Well you simply must read his book about Hawaii. Night Marchers, the spirit of Pele, murderers who disappear in the jungles. It's all terribly thrilling.

"Maybe I'll check it out," Cindy said, mostly just to get the woman to change topics.

"Cindy!"

She glanced over her shoulder just as Al walked up. He was carrying a long, red flotation device with straps at either end. "I grabbed you one of these. Everyone else is in the water; you just have to go."

"I don't swim," Cindy said.

"Oh, come on everyone can swim."

"Not me. I won't." It was true. It wasn't that she couldn't swim. She absolutely would not swim.

"Look, we have these nice life preserves, floaties, they go around your waist and keep you on top of the water. It does all the work so all you have to do is stare at fish. Some of the best snorkeling in all the world is right here. You'll see fish you won't see anywhere else."

Cindy wished he'd let it go, but apparently he took his job very seriously.

"I really don't want to. I just want to sit here and relax, no stress for me. That's more work than I want to do right now," she said, hoping to appeal to his island spirit. "You know, hang loose."

"You just jump off the back of the boat. What could be easier?"

She felt her stomach clench and she could taste bile in her mouth. "No," she whispered fiercely.

He raised his hands and backed away slowly.

"You one crazy wahine, you know that?" he asked.

"Well I know *this* wahine feels like getting a little crazy," Marge said, standing up. "You've talked me into it."

She reached for the life preserver he was holding.

"We'll leave this one for her in case she changes her mind. I'll get you a different one," he offered.

"Nonsense. You heard the girl. She's not going in the water."

Marge grabbed the life preserver and he looked like he wanted to argue with her but instead just shook his head and walked away.

Cindy relaxed back into the chair and closed her eyes, trying to drink up the sunlight as Marge and Al headed for the back of the boat. She could feel the sun beating down on her, warming her through to her bones. She began to drowse, her mind slipping lazily from one thought to another.

A scream of terror shattered the air.

4

Detective Mark Walters felt like he had bearded the lion in his den. The man sitting across from him was staring at him, daggers in his eyes. The silence that stretched between them was thick with tension.

The weeks since his suspension from the police department had been a living nightmare, but it all paled in comparison to the danger he felt like he was in at that moment.

"Look, I'm sorry I hauled you down here on your day off, but I don't like this anymore than you do," Mark growled, breaking the silence first and trying not to feel like that meant he had lost.

Rabbi Jeremiah Silverman was still glowering at him. "I'm not *your* rabbi."

"Yeah, but you're the closest thing to a rabbi or a priest or whatever that I've got. And I'll be hanged if I am going to go spill my guts to the department shrink," Mark said.

They were sitting in Jeremiah's office in the synagogue. The place was officially closed for the weekend which was how Mark had wanted it. He didn't need Jeremiah's secretary knowing why he was there.

"I could refuse to sign off on your psych evaluation," Jeremiah said, staring stonily at him.

"And I could start asking how a crazy mother like you became a rabbi," Mark said.

He watched closely to see if his remark hit home. If it did, the rabbi refused to show it, face remaining inscrutable.

"Take your shot," he said with a shrug. "Though I'm not sure how your supervisors will feel about it."

Jeremiah had called his bluff.

Mark sighed and leaned forward. "Look, just cut the crap. The department won't even think about reinstating me without a psych evaluation and mandatory hours of therapy."

"How many?"

"Too many. The point is —"

"The point is you think I'll just let you off easy."

"I was hoping so," Mark said, locking his jaw.

Jeremiah leaned forward. His eyes looked tired, but there was a determined air about him. "Look, Mark. If you insist on doing this there's no holding back here. You're right, as a rabbi I do have counseling experience which can be called upon in these types of circumstances. But I won't give you a pass. If you come to me for the hours, you're going to have to put in the effort. It's both our jobs if we don't do this right."

Mark slumped in his chair. Jeremiah was right, he just didn't want to hear it. He'd already had four sessions with the department psychologist, enough to know that he didn't trust the guy to be the one deciding his fate. And he wasn't someone he had any intention of spilling his guts to ever.

"Fine."

"Okay, we can start now."

"Now?"

"Unless you're not serious," Jeremiah said, lacing his fingers together.

"Need I remind you that I did what I did to save your skin?" Mark demanded.

"And I want you to rest assured that that will have no bearing whatsoever on my assessment of your ability to do your job."

"Bastard."

Jeremiah smirked. "No, but I've been called worse."

"I bet you have."

Mark leaned back in his chair. "Okay, let's get this over with."

"Okay. Tell me what happened in that interrogation room."

Mark could feel the bile rising in the back of his throat. He shut his eyes, wishing he could block the memories as easily. He balled his fists in frustration. Jeremiah wasn't going to pull any punches or beat around the bush.

Fine. I asked for this. For him.

"I realized that he was the only one who might be able to call off the hit. Your life, the lives of those kids, stacked up to a lot more than this man's rights."

"And to more than your duties and responsibilities as a police officer."

Mark opened his eyes and stared at him, rage roiling inside him. "It's my duty and responsibility to protect and serve. I was *protecting* all of you. I was doing the city a *service.*"

"And you tortured a man because you felt you had to."

"Yes."

Jeremiah raised an eyebrow and Mark silently cursed, wishing he knew what to say, what answers would get him out of trouble and back on the job.

But there was a long way to go and so many questions.

"What can I say? Sometimes the needs of the many outweigh the needs of the few. I made a decision and I stand by it."

"You stand by it. You'd make it again?"

"Yes."

"But can you live with it?"

Mark could feel himself beginning to sweat. He felt like the rabbi was staring right through him, piercing his very soul.

"I have nightmares," he whispered, feeling like he was having to wrest the words free. He hadn't admitted that to anyone, not even his wife, even though she surely knew. He awoke most mornings screaming, images of the man's bloody face swimming in front of him.

"I'm sure that you do."

"Look, I believe absolutely that it was the right decision."

"But just because you believe it was right doesn't make it easy to live with."

"No," he admitted. "I wish I never had to make it. I wish it had been Paul at the precinct, me heading to the mountains to try and help."

"So, you wish you were dead instead of sitting here?"

And it sounded so terrible coming from

the rabbi's lips that way. But heaven help him, it was true. He could have died a hero and he wouldn't have had to drag his wife through this hell with him.

And I would never have known Paul was lying to me, that he wasn't who he said he was.

The mystery of his partner's true identity still hadn't been solved. The coroner was the only one who had discussed it with him. Knowing that the man he'd called Paul Dryer wasn't, that the real Paul Dryer was in a mass grave at Green Pastures camp haunted him.

It felt like his entire career was a house of cards that someone had knocked over with a single breath, like blowing out a candle.

No, not someone. Me. I did this to myself.

And he had been over it a thousand times in his head and he knew that Paul had known exactly what Mark would do, pushed the right buttons to ensure that Mark would do exactly what he did.

"Did I do the right thing?" he whispered, hearing the heartache in his own voice.

Jeremiah stared at him for what seemed like an eternity. When he spoke again his voice was also softer, and he could hear compassion in it. "What we're here to discuss is how *you* feel, how you think, and whether that makes you fit for duty or not.

What I believe, what the department believes, these are not the issue. The only opinion I'm here to give is on whether or not I think you can safely return to your duties as a police officer without putting yourself or others in jeopardy. And until we're done, you won't hear me voice opinions on anything else."

"That wasn't designed to make me feel good," Mark said.

Jeremiah cleared his throat. "That's not my job."

Cindy jumped to her feet as the scream was suddenly cut short. She ran over to the starboard side of the boat. The scream seemed to have been coming from that direction.

She looked over the side and for a moment saw nothing. Then she made out a disturbance in the water close to the back of the boat. The water was being churned up and she saw two hands disappear below the surface.

"Help! Someone's drowning!" she shouted at the top of her lungs. "Starboard side! Help!"

One of the crew members raced her way and without a moment's hesitation threw himself over the railing and into the ocean.

He dove under and Cindy watched the spot where he and the passenger had disappeared anxiously.

Seconds drug by and her heart began to pound harder and fear flooded her. Her fingers hurt where she was squeezing the railing with an iron grip. Another crew member reached her.

"Where?" he shouted.

She pointed with a shaking finger and he, too, dove into the water. Before he could go under, though, the first rescuer broke the surface with a gasp. A moment later she could see Marge's head as he pulled her up. The two guys supported her and swam toward the back of the boat.

Cindy raced around and was there when they pulled Marge up into the boat. The older woman was coughing up water and shaking uncontrollably. Someone quickly wrapped a blanket around her.

"What happened to her floatation device?" she heard someone ask.

The crew member who'd rescued her shook his head. "There was something wrong with it. I had to cut it free. I lost my dive knife, too."

Cindy followed as they moved Marge to a chair. The woman had begun to sob.

"Her husband's still in the water," Cindy

said. "Someone should get him."

"I'm on it," a familiar voice said.

She glanced at Al sideways before returning her attention to the distraught woman.

"You're going to be okay," she said to Marge, laying a hand on her arm.

The other woman shook her head. "It was terrible. I thought I was going to drown."

"But you didn't. You're safe now," Cindy said, in what she hoped was a soothing voice.

"For a minute everything was fine and I was looking at the fish and thinking it wasn't so bad and I was glad I did it. Then it started pulling me under!"

Cindy felt the hair raise on the back of her neck. "Something pulled you under? What was it?" she asked.

"It was that stupid belt. It nearly killed me!"

"The floatation belt?" Cindy asked. "The one Al gave you?"

"That's the one. It just suddenly got so heavy and it was sinking and I couldn't fight it and I couldn't get it to unbuckle. And then . . . and then I was underwater."

Marge began to cry harder and Cindy rubbed her back, making gentle sounds even as her own mind was racing.

Al had wanted her to go in the water, had

wanted her to wear that floatation device. If she had it would be her sitting where Marge was.

Unless no one figured out where I was in time, she realized with a shiver. It had been her screams for help that had brought the crewmen to rescue Marge. She felt like she was going to be sick.

The ocean that had looked so beautiful and serene just minutes ago now looked ugly and dangerous to her. She wanted nothing more than for them to turn the boat around and get back to dry land as soon as possible.

"Marge!"

She looked up and saw an older man rushing toward them, his face contorted in fear.

"Marge, are you all right?" he gasped as he dropped down beside the woman and wrapped his arms around her.

Cindy didn't know if Marge actually answered him or just burst into tears again. She stood up and moved back a few feet trying to give the couple their space. She looked around and noticed that nearly everyone seemed to be back onboard the catamaran.

Ten minutes later they were on their way back to the port. A crewmember had explained that everyone onboard was going to be given a voucher for a free excursion since the trip was being cut short. They wanted to get back as quickly as possible so that Marge could be checked out by a physician. Cindy privately thought they should also be checking out all their safety equipment at the same time.

The mood back was incredibly subdued as even the unaffected passengers seemed to be speaking in hushed tones. Death, or even a close call, could do that to people. It subdued and sobered. That was what it had done to her so many years before.

Her brother, Kyle, came to mind. A brush with death had had the opposite affect on him. If anything it had made him louder, more exuberant, more reckless. She'd never been able to understand his attitude or truly forgive him for it.

Cindy stood up and walked the length of the boat to stretch her legs. She kept careful hold of the railing as she did so. As she moved to the bow of the ship she realized that she was looking for Al. The thought of him holding out the faulty life preserver to her hadn't left her mind and she wished she could ask him a few questions about it.

Al, however, was nowhere to be seen. He must have been with the captain. Disappointed she made it all the way around the catamaran and back to her seat near Marge and her husband.

Marge seemed to have stopped crying but both she and her husband still looked pale and shaken. Cindy couldn't blame them. Neither could she help but wonder if either of them would ever venture into the water again. Somehow she doubted it. Marge didn't seem like a get-back-on-the-horse kind of person.

Not that I should judge, she thought sadly. There were so many things that the death of her sister had kept her from doing. If she was honest with herself there were times where she almost envied Kyle. His freedom and uninhibited joy in life were two things she could only dream of. Still, as the life preserver incident illustrated, her fears and limitations could very well be all that had kept her alive over the years.

When they made it back to the dock there was an ambulance waiting for Marge. She protested that she was fine but ultimately relented and allowed herself to be whisked away to the hospital. Cindy huddled with the other passengers waiting to be given their vouchers and sent on their way.

She kept looking for Al, but she didn't see him. That perplexed her a bit. Maybe he was too embarrassed to show his face given that he was the one who'd handed Marge the faulty life preserver. He shouldn't be embarrassed. It was an accident. It could have happened to anyone.

What if it wasn't an accident?

Cindy blinked as the thought entered her mind unbidden. It was ridiculous. She couldn't even fathom how one would go about sabotaging one of those life preservers. And besides, who would possibly want to hurt Marge?

Then she remembered how Al had tried to discourage Marge from taking that particular life preserver, wanting instead to leave it for Cindy.

What if he, or someone else, was trying to hurt me?

She shivered and wrapped her arms around herself.

Crazy. Paranoid. That's what she was. There was no possible reason anyone, least of all some stranger on a tour in Hawaii, would want to harm her. She was just jumpy. Too many brushes with death and danger had made her that way. It was exactly why she needed this vacation.

I have to relax, she told herself. *If I'm spooking this easy here, imagine how much worse it will be when I'm back home.*

She dug into her purse for her cell phone.

She wanted to call Jeremiah. She froze, though. What could he do other than tell her to stop looking for killers under every rock? She hesitated, still wanting to talk to him.

Finally she dialed his phone. It rang four times then went to voicemail. She hesitated and then hung up. No need to alarm him needlessly.

At last a crewmember handed her a voucher and said she was free to go. She crammed it into her purse and headed for the van that would take her bac k to her hotel.

Several other passengers crammed in with her and a minute later they were off. Cindy was relieved that hers was the first stop. She had to crawl across two other passengers to get out of the van but she finally made it. Once on the street she opted for some more shopping and sightseeing. She still had several hours before dinner and she wanted to make the most of them.

For lunch she grabbed a pineapple Dole Whip from a small stand and ate it as she walked. She bought a flower for her hair and carefully fastened it on the right side of her head as she was instructed. Flower on the right side was single; flower on the left side was taken.

"Let all young men know you in the market," the woman who sold the flower to her told her with a thick accent.

It made Cindy blush. She wasn't shopping for a guy while on vacation. That would be long-distance crazy making. In the next moment she thought of her dinner with the detective and blushed harder, much to the delight of the flower vendor. She shook her head. What would Jeremiah say?

Things were quiet without Cindy around, Jeremiah realized. He walked into his house and gave Captain a quick pat on the head. He kept expecting to see Cindy or hear from her in some way. The conversation with Mark had shaken him more than he liked and he wanted someone to talk to.

Not that he'd ever talk to Cindy about counseling Mark. Not only would that violate Mark's privacy, it would also open a whole can of worms that he wasn't ready to deal with yet.

You should tell her who you are, a voice seemed to whisper in his head.

Who I was, he corrected the voice. *That's not who I am anymore.*

The still small voice didn't seem to believe that anymore than he did.

He took out his wallet and phone and

74

deposited them on the dresser in his bedroom. He picked his phone back up and checked it. His heart lifted a little when he saw that he had missed a call from Cindy. She hadn't left a message.

He was about to call her back when he stopped himself. She was on vacation and he had promised himself he wouldn't disturb her while she was gone. If she hadn't left him a message it couldn't be anything important. For all he knew she had dialed the number by accident before hanging up.

He sighed and put the phone back down. He stared grimly at his reflection in the mirror. *Why did things have to be so complicated?*

Captain padded into the room and whined deep in his throat. Jeremiah patted him. "Not the way I wanted to spend my day off either, boy."

The dog dropped a tennis ball at Jeremiah's feet. Jeremiah sighed as he picked it up. "You want to go to the park and play, don't you?"

The dog wagged his tail as though he understood and whined again.

"Okay," Jeremiah relented, wishing there was a better place he could take the dog to play fetch. For a brief moment he thought of Cindy's friend Joseph who had the sprawling estate and acres of grass for his own beloved dog to run around on. No matter how he practiced it in his own head, though, there was no way in which asking Joseph to borrow his lawn didn't seem suspicious.

"The park it is," he told Captain.

Jeremiah changed quickly into jogging shorts and a T-shirt and then piled with the big dog into his car. Twenty minutes later they were running around, tossing the ball, and Jeremiah was enjoying the exercise every bit as much as Captain was. Maybe he worried too much, he reasoned. Maybe he was too cautious.

After all, it had to have been coincidence that Captain's former owner frequented this park even though it was in the very town Jeremiah had set up residence, nearly halfway around the globe from the place they had last seen each other.

"Stranger things have happened," he told Captain as the dog danced around, eagerly waiting for him to throw the ball again.

He tossed it long and then raced Captain, who beat him easily to the ball. He got down on the ground and wrestled with the dog who was just in heaven. Finally he got the ball away from him and threw it again, this time letting Captain do all the running and bring it back to him.

After they were both good and winded Jeremiah led Captain over to some tables and benches in the shade. Sometimes people could be found there playing chess, but apparently everyone else had something better to do at that point.

Except for one man, sitting, a chess board neatly arranged in front of him as though he was waiting for someone. As Jeremiah approached he got a strange, twisting sensation in his gut and as the man looked up and smiled at him he realized the man had been waiting for someone.

Him.

5

Jeremiah was standing, staring at the old man who had come up to him the day before, the one who had said it was urgent they talk and had scheduled an appointment with him for Wednesday.

Marie was right to be concerned, the words flashed through his mind.

"Sit," the man said, indicating the empty chair across from him. "We have much to talk about."

Jeremiah turned and quickly scanned the surrounding environment, looking for anything that was out of place . . . like the fact that no one else was near them in the park and the other tables that usually housed chess players sat empty. He was a fool for not having been suspicious earlier.

A very old habit drove his hand to the back of his waistband, but there was nothing there to grab. He had no weapons to aid him.

The old man chuckled. "Do not worry. I paid the others who were sitting here to go away and leave us alone for a few minutes."

"An awful lot of work and money wasted when you could have just kept our appointment on Wednesday.

The old man shrugged. "I am . . . how do you say? An opportunist. When opportunity presents itself, I act upon it. Much like you, I think."

Jeremiah shook his head. "I don't know what you're talking about."

The other cocked his head, regarding him long and steadily. Jeremiah stood his ground, his mask firmly in place, revealing nothing through his eyes, his facial expressions. Finally the man shrugged. "Perhaps I am wrong, but that does not change the fact that we need to talk. Sit, play a game with an old man."

It could be a trap. The chair could have a bomb rigged to it or there could be an accomplice just waiting somewhere to pick him off the moment he did. "How did you know I would come here," he asked, stalling for time.

"I didn't. I came for the chess. And then I saw you and your beautiful dog. German Shepherds are a wonderful breed. Here is the best shade and a drinking fountain for both man and beast. I figured it likely you would come over."

Slowly Jeremiah sat down even though he still wasn't convinced this wasn't a trap. Captain laid down at his side, keeping a watchful eye on him. He could tell the dog sensed his apprehension and was just waiting to be told what the problem was.

"You are white. It is your move first."

Jeremiah slid one of his pawns forward, still keeping an eye on the older man. "How about you tell me your name?"

"You may call me Otto," the man said as he pushed forward one of his own pawns.

"What do you want with me, Otto?" Jeremiah asked, moving his knight.

"I need your help with something."

Again Jeremiah looked around, sure that they must be being watched by someone. He turned back and picked up with the game, listening, waiting.

"I am a very old man and my time is running short. I want to make amends. You understand this, ja?"

"I'm not sure what you think it is I can do for you. If you're looking for absolution, you might try a priest of some sort."

"Nein. Not absolution. Restoration."

"I'm afraid you're going to have to be a lot more clear than that."

It was Otto's turn to look around, and there was a fearfulness to him that gave Jeremiah pause. Maybe the man really was in trouble and looking for his help.

"Möchtest Du spazieren gehen?"

"In English, please," Jeremiah said, refusing to give any sign that he'd understood the man.

"Would you like to go for a walk?"

"Okay," Jeremiah said, rising swiftly. Captain quickly followed suit and stood looking at him, waiting for instruction.

Otto began to walk slowly away from the table, leaving the chess game half finished. Jeremiah joined him with Captain pressing close to his legs.

"I can never help the people I should. It is impossible. But I have determined that I can help someone else. I want to help you, your synagogue. It will go a small way toward righting a great wrong, to repaying a great debt."

Jeremiah was beginning to wonder if maybe Otto was suffering from some kind of dementia instead of trying to be deliberately evasive.

He reached out and touched the old man's arm and Otto jerked as though he had been scalded.

Jeremiah let his hand fall away. "Otto, if

81

you need my help, you're going to have to be very clear and explain to me exactly what it is that you're talking about."

Otto stared up at the sky, whether seeking wisdom or some sort of sign Jeremiah couldn't tell. Finally he turned and looked him in the eyes. Otto's eyes were clear, thought quickening in them, not the eyes of someone who wasn't clear what was going on.

"I will trust you and I will do as you say, but Wednesday when we are scheduled to meet. I will bring something then to show you. Something very important and when you see it, you will understand everything."

Jeremiah realized that he was now completely intrigued and even though every cell of his being urged him to walk away he stood his ground. "I'm free the rest of the day. Is there somewhere you want to go to talk more now?"

"Nein. It will take me a day to retrieve what it is I must show you. Now, I have taken up too much of your day already. Go, enjoy. Have a thoughtful and peaceful Memorial Day tomorrow and I will see you on Wednesday."

The old man turned and started walking away. His back was straight, his head was up, and his steps were sure. He walked without wavering, heading off to wherever it was he was going. Jeremiah stood and watched him out of sight. Otto was a man with a purpose.

And I guess on Wednesday I'll find out what it is.

Cindy gingerly smeared aloe onto the red skin of her arms and winced. It was her own fault for not reapplying sunscreen halfway through the day. Finished with that she grabbed the little black dress that Geanie had insisted she bring with her "just in case".

The dress was, in fact, Geanie's. Fortunately it wasn't too outlandish given her roommate's penchant for crazy clothes. It had a halter top and came down to her knees. She slipped on her sandals because the only other shoes she had brought with her were tennis shoes. After applying light makeup she examined herself in the mirror. Except for her red arms she looked pretty good.

She picked up her purse and felt her nerves begin to spiral out of control. She grabbed the deck of cards she'd bought the day before off of the dresser and shoved them in her purse. In case she needed to, she could always fidget with them under the table and hopefully he wouldn't notice.

She left her room and walked to the elevator, feeling even more nervous. She wasn't good at dating and lately it seemed like most of the men who asked her out were either completely wrong for her or murderers.

I guess I have every right to be nervous, she told herself.

In the lobby Kapono was already waiting for her dressed in slacks and a Hawaiian shirt. She had learned that this constituted formal wear for the islands. He flashed her an appreciative smile and she dipped her head in acknowledgement.

"I thought you'd be on island time," she admitted. "I was sure I'd have at least another ten minutes."

"We move slow most of the time because we don't feel like rushing," he admitted. "But we can still move quickly if we see something we want."

She didn't know what to say to that and wished she'd never made the joke in the first place.

As if sensing her discomfort he gave a slow, easy laugh. "You need to loosen up. Good food can help with that; let's go."

He took her to a seafood restaurant that was little more than a shack on a stretch of beach she hadn't seen yet. As they were being seated the sun was already beginning to set and Cindy couldn't help but marvel at the colors that blazed across the sky.

"Is beautiful, no?"

"Yes," she told him. "Thank you. I would never have found this place on my own."

He grinned. "You know the best part?"

"What?" she asked.

"Since we're on the sand you can kick off your shoes."

She laughed, caught off guard. She glanced under the table and saw that he had indeed discarded his sandals.

"Come on, go native," he urged with an engaging grin.

After a moment's hesitation she kicked off her sandals and dug her toes into the warm sand.

"See, mo' better."

"Mo' better," she agreed.

She picked up her menu and discovered that all it had listed were a couple of appetizers and then several different ways that they could prepare fish. The lemon caper butter sauce sounded amazing.

"What fish do they have?" she asked, trying to figure out the menu.

"The waiter will tell us what they have today. Then you pick how you want it cooked and what sauce you want."

A minute later the waiter appeared. "Good evening. Before we get started I'll just let you know about our fish tonight. First we have ono which is a mild fish with a firm texture."

"Ono also means good in Hawaiian," Kapono said with a grin.

"Yes. The ono is very ono," the waiter said with a grin. "Next we have mahi mahi which is a firm white fish with a sweet flavor. I recommend it with the coconut and macadamia nut crust. Finally tonight we have monchong —"

"Say no more," Kapono said, interrupting with a raised hand. He looked at Cindy. "Have you had monchong?"

"No."

"Then you will tonight. I'll take mine sautéed in the lemon caper butter sauce."

"Better make that two," Cindy said, handing the waiter her menu.

"I promise you will not be disappointed," the waiter said before heading off.

"Monchong must be a specialty," she ventured once he had gone.

"You've never tasted anything to beat it," Kapono said. "Trust me on this."

"Well, if you can't trust a detective, who can you trust?" she joked.

But even as the words left her mouth she

86

couldn't help but think about the corrupt police officer she had helped capture half a year before. Still, he hadn't been a detective. She forced herself to smile, hoping Kapono didn't notice her sudden tension.

The waiter brought them some water and she hastily began to sip hers, trying to cover for herself while she tried to force herself to calm down. Finally she put the glass down.

"How was the rest of your day yesterday, see anything interesting?" he asked, picking up his own water glass.

"You mean, more interesting than a dead body?"

He choked on his water and then set the glass down carefully. "Hopefully more pleasant at least."

She couldn't resist the urge to tease him. "Well, I did see another dead body yesterday evening."

His eyes nearly bulged out of his head. "You gotta be kidding me."

"Nope."

"What happened?" he asked.

"I went to a luau on the north shore. I was walking on the beach before dinner and I saw some people moving one of the bodies on that proposed resort site I've been hearing about."

He winced. "I'm sorry."

She shrugged. "At least it wasn't as . . . traumatic . . . as the other one."

"I'm sorry again."

"So, have you caught the person who killed Uncle yet?"

"Excuse me?" he asked, sounding surprised.

She grimaced. "Sorry, it's just, clearly that's been on my mind a lot."

"No, that's okay. It's understandable that you'd be curious and concerned. We don't have anyone in custody yet, but we are following up on all leads."

"It's just so terrible. Some nice old guy has a little restaurant business and then somebody does that to him."

Kapono chuckled.

"What's so funny?"

"Hearing you describe him as a nice old guy."

"I thought he was like an uncle to everyone."

"Oh yes, he certainly was. Uncle could always help you with your problems . . . for a price."

"What does that mean?" she asked, leaning forward intently.

"Nothing," he said, waving a hand dismissively.

"It didn't sound like nothing. Come on,

I'm leaving the day after tomorrow and I'm going to have to live with those images the rest of my life."

He sobered. "I'm sorry that you're trip to our island has been so tainted."

She took a deep breath, sensing that she could get him to talk if she went slow.

"I'm sad too. I guess if I understood it more it would help me put it in perspective, not taint my entire image and all my memories of this place."

Inwardly Cindy winced. It sounded so contrived. But she deeply wanted to know what had happened to the restaurateur.

"I'm not sure knowing any more would actually help you feel better," he said with a sad grimace.

She reached out and put a hand on his. "I know it would," she urged.

"Okay. We have drug problems here, same as anywhere on the mainland. Some small businesses, the occasional restaurant, owe ninety-percent of their business to the fact that they can help launder the money from illegal activities."

Cindy felt like her eyes must be bulging out of her head. "Really?"

He nodded.

"And Uncle's was one of those places?"

"We've suspected for some time that it

was. He was staying in business somehow and trust me, it had nothing to do with the food. You're lucky you didn't get to eat there."

"But my taxi driver told me it was some of the best food on the island, insisted that I should go there after I visited Pearl Harbor.

"What? Are you sure?" he asked, leaning forward abruptly as his eyes quickened with thought.

"Yes. That's the only reason I was there, the only way I found it. When he dropped me at Pearl Harbor he even showed me how to walk so I could get there."

A pad and a pen appeared as if by magic in Kapono's hands. "I should have thought to wonder how you ended up there. It wasn't exactly on the beaten path for tourists. In fact, Uncle was the kind who definitely didn't encourage tourists to come to his place. More of a 'locals only' kind of guy. Do you know the name of the taxi driver?"

"No, but it was a Wiki Taxi. Maybe they have a record of picking me up at my hotel yesterday morning."

"Maybe," he said, hastily scribbling on his notepad. "Can you describe the driver?"

Cindy did to the best of her abilities but

90

was afraid from the look on Kapono's face that she'd just described a third of the native population.

"If we need to, do you think I could get you to work with a sketch artist tomorrow?"

"Sure. I take it the driver is important?" she said, eager to know what he was thinking.

"Could be. Makes no sense that he'd send you there, though. He didn't say anything else, give you anything?"

"No, nothing like that," Cindy said. Her blood was beginning to quicken and she couldn't help the thrill that flashed through her. Another mystery to solve.

But, you're going home, she reminded herself. *This has nothing to do with you. Just let it go.*

But with the next breath she realized that she didn't want to let it go. And then she remembered that she did have something. "Hold on, I forgot, but he gave me a business card."

"Great."

She fished in her purse and found the card. She handed it to him. He frowned as he studied it, turning it over.

"This doesn't look like a Wiki Taxi business card."

"He said if I needed anything he could

take good care of me. Maybe he freelances on the side and his boss doesn't know it?" she suggested.

"Maybe. We'll check it out."

When did I become this girl? she couldn't help but wonder. Solving crimes was anything but safe. In fact, so far it had turned out to be far more dangerous than all the crazy stunts her brother pulled.

"Excuse me for just a minute," Kapono said.

He stood and moved several yards away so he wouldn't be overheard. She could see him talking on his phone and wished she knew how to read lips. A couple of minutes later he returned.

"Sorry," he said. "I have my partner tracking down your driver. Hopefully it will be the break we need."

"I hope so," she said.

He hesitated. "I'm sorry. This is awkward. I should never have asked you out. Normally I wouldn't ask out a witness, but you're a very attractive woman and given how soon you're leaving the island I figured it was now or never."

She couldn't help the smile that stretched across her face. He thought she was attractive. "Thank you."

"It's my bad."

"No worries," she said. "Look. We might as well finish dinner. If you want to bounce thoughts off me great. If not, that's fine too. But apparently I can't leave the island without trying monchong, so . . ."

"Now that would truly be a crime."

"So monchong it is," she said with a grin.

"And while we wait you can tell me how your day today went," he said, clearly trying to steer her off the murder.

"I went on one of those snorkel cruises. It was crazy. A woman almost drowned because something was wrong with her flotation device."

His eyes again grew enormous. "I heard about that. You were on that boat?"

"Yeah, one of the crew kept trying to convince me to go in the water, he even handed me that flotation device, but there was no way I was going in."

Kapono raised an eyebrow. "You went on a snorkel cruise not to snorkel."

She shrugged. "I wanted to go out *on* the water. I didn't necessarily want to go *in* the water. And I got to see some dolphins, so that was cool."

"And had you gone in the water you would have been the one to almost drown."

"I guess so," she said, a shiver running up her spine.

Kapono wiped a hand across his face. "Do things like this happen to you at home or just here?"

She hesitated. "Well, maybe a couple of things, but certainly usually not in this high a concentration."

He groaned. "So you come to the land of aloha for a nice vacation and instead you're living a tourist's nightmare."

She shrugged. "At least I got to meet some nice people."

"Like me?"

"Yes, and the lady on the boat, she was quite sweet and a couple at the luau last night."

Kapono shook his head. "That's messed up."

Cindy smiled. "Well, hopefully nothing will happen tonight but the eating of some amazing fish."

"Amen to that sistah," he said.

When the food came Cindy had to admit it was one of the most delicious things she had ever eaten. Kapono didn't want to talk about the case and she had to grudgingly respect him for his professionalism. He talked about the island and its history instead and she listened, fascinated. She realized she definitely was going to just barely scratch the surface in her few days there and it made her want to come back and spend some real time getting to know the island and its people.

Her mind kept drifting back to the murder, though, and what he had told her about uncle. That 'locals only' comment reminded her of some of the ones she'd heard on the radio. It made her a little sad, but she still wanted to know who killed him. If what Kapono said was true, it was probably a drug dealer, someone Uncle did business with. She thought of the women in the food-court at the International Marketplace. They had been saying that Uncle was mixed up with bad people. Apparently they were right.

At the end of the evening Kapono drove her back to her hotel and said goodnight. She waved as he drove off.

She headed up the escalator to the lobby and from there got on the elevator. She couldn't help but think about what she had learned about Uncle as she exited and walked to her room.

You're leaving in thirty-six hours. You don't have time to get involved any more than you already are, she told herself sternly.

Cindy walked into her room and stopped. Something was very wrong. She spun around and reached for the door. A hand clamped over her mouth, pressing a rag with a foul-smelling liquid to her face.

The world swam in front of her and then everything went black.

6

Mark sighed as he parked in his driveway. It had been a long, frustrating day. The high point had turned out to be his meeting with Jeremiah. Things had just gone downhill from there. He had tried again unsuccessfully to interview some of Paul's family members and then done a dozen of the errands Traci seemed to have for him to do now that he had more free time on his hands.

The day had ended with a retirement party for one of his friends on the force. Despite his misgivings he had been talked into attending. Words like "show them you're not ashamed" and "remind people that you're around" had been thrown at him to get him to go.

And fifteen minutes into the party he wished he hadn't reminded people that he was still around. Cops who screwed up like he had became like lepers. No one wanted to get near them for fear that the bad behavior and subsequent department trouble were catching.

Still he had sat through the whole thing, gritting his teeth even as he tried to smile at his colleagues as though he hadn't heard what they were saying about him. They could have at least had the courtesy to gossip out of his earshot. But where would have been the fun in that.

He walked into the house, not bothering to turn on the lights. He had told Traci not to wait up for him.

The light in the bedroom was on and he trudged toward it wearily, struggling to find a smile for her sake. From the look on her face when he came into the room he gathered he'd managed to form more of a grimace than a smile.

"Rough day?" she asked.

And even those two little words killed him a little. Whenever he'd drug himself home in bad shape before she'd always asked: *Rough day at work?*

But now the last two words were gone. There was no more at work because there was no work. They had enough in savings to float them for a couple of more months but that wasn't what bothered him. What bothered him was the one more tiny reminder that he had screwed up and because of it he had no work to go to.

He hadn't expected the department to dangle the carrot of possibly bringing him back into the fold. Frankly, he'd expected to be in jail by now. Nights like this, though, the carrot seemed more taunt than promise.

"Yeah, rough day," he said finally as he kicked off his shoes.

"Did the rabbi agree to do it?" Traci asked.

Mark nodded.

"Well, that's a relief, isn't it?"

He sat down on the bed. "Yeah, I guess."

"What's wrong?" she asked, eyes filled with concern.

"He's going to make me work for it. And he's going to push me harder than I want to be pushed."

She bit her lip. She always did that when she was debating whether or not to say something.

"What?" he asked.

"Maybe it will be good for you."

Mark sighed. "That's what I'm afraid of."

He was hard enough on himself every day without having to talk about it with someone else, feel their judgment and condemnation.

"It's going to be okay," she said.

He wanted to believe her so badly. He

wanted, *needed,* everything to be okay again.

She began rubbing his shoulders and he sighed and closed his eyes.

The world was spinning, rocking, and Cindy's stomach clenched. As she started to come awake she could hear a droning noise as well.

What's happened to me? she wondered, trying to force her eyes open.

Total darkness greeted her. She blinked rapidly several times but even though she could feel that her eyes were opening only darkness remained.

Panic surged through her and she tried to sit up only to realize she couldn't. She struggled to grasp what was happening. She was blind and she couldn't move. Had she been in some terrible accident?

Then the rest of her senses kicked in. She could feel something coarse in her mouth which she couldn't spit out. Her hands were behind her back and she could feel something hard digging into them. When she touched them together she could hear the clink of metal. Something scratchy was binding her legs together.

Handcuffed, gagged, blindfolded. With a rush she remembered the rag that had been clamped over her mouth when she'd walked into her hotel room.

I've been kidnapped.

Fresh terror gripped her. Her stomach churned and she thought she was going to be sick. The motion she had felt earlier was real. She could smell gasoline mixed with the salty smell of the ocean.

I must be on a boat.

Which meant that no one would have any idea where to look for her.

She thrashed about, kicking out at anything and everything. She heard a few dull thuds and then a sharp pain stabbed through her wrists. She stopped moving. Her heart was hammering and she struggled to get as much air as she could. Her lungs were burning from lack of oxygen which sent fresh waves of panic through her.

Her wrists were throbbing and she prayed she hadn't broken anything a moment after praying that she would be found and rescued. She lay still, trying to regain her wits as her body calmed down.

She was on a boat, but where? And who had kidnapped her? Faces flashed through her mind: Al, her taxi driver, Kapono. What could any one of them possibly want from her? She couldn't help but wonder if her being kidnapped was somehow related to the murder of Uncle.

She wanted to scream that she didn't know anything, she was just a tourist. The best she could make out around the gag was a garbled sob. Tears stung her eyes and she fiercely tried to push them away. She had to keep calm if she wanted to survive this.

That was going to be easier said than done though. Especially since she was gagged and getting seasick. She lay still, trying to listen to see if she could hear anyone talking. There was only the sound of the boat's engine, though.

She wondered how long she had been unconscious. Her feet were tingling like they were falling asleep and she struggled to move them.

After what seemed like forever the sound of the engine changed and the motion of the boat seemed to slow. A moment later it began to rock harder. They had to be stopping.

Every muscle in her body tensed. Soon she would be face-to-face with her kidnappers. She wished she knew how to escape from her restraints or fight back. Instead she lay there, helpless, waiting for them to come for her.

The boat stopped moving and the engine powered down. After a moment she heard heavy footsteps and then a shout. Were they in port?

Then she heard two men speaking. One was very soft spoken and the other louder.

". . . problem . . ."

"What did you do about it?"

The other man answered, but she couldn't make out his words. She strained to listen, hoping to hear something that could help her.

"What are you, stupid? Why'd you bring her here?"

". . . think she has . . ."

"Then take it from her and get rid of her."

She jerked, smacking her head on something and she reeled for a moment, trying to keep herself from blacking out.

"Get it done."

She heard footsteps fading away. A moment later she heard another set and they were coming close to her. The boat creaked and she heard the sound of a door opening.

Someone was close by. She could hear them moving.

"Okay, time to get down to business."

It was the man with the softer voice.

A hand wrapped around her arm and she jumped and screamed. The sound was severely muted because of the gag. She thrashed around but his grip tightened and he pulled her along a rough floor, scratching her bare legs.

He grabbed her other arm and hauled her to her feet. She swayed, still bound and unable to get her balance. He shoved her hard in the chest and she fell backward. She braced herself for the impact but was jarred when it came sooner than expected.

She had landed in some kind of chair. Her handcuffed hands took the brunt of her weight and were crushed between her body and the chair. She could feel the steel biting into her skin even harder and something warm and sticky started running over her hands. Moments later she smelled the blood. Her stomach clenched harder and she was sure she was going to be sick.

"Now, where is it?" the man demanded.

Unable to speak around the gag she shook her head violently side-to-side. Where was what? What could he possibly be looking for?

"I'm going to take off the gag, but if you try to scream again I'm going to slit your throat. Do you understand?"

She nodded.

Metal touched her cheek and she jerked back.

Pain exploded across her cheek and she heard the ring of a slap. "Stupid wahine, sit still," he barked.

The metal touched her cheek again and slid between her skin and the cloth of the gag. There was the sound of ripping fabric and the gag came free. She spat it out of her mouth.

"I don't know what you want, please let me go!" she begged.

"Don't play games with me. I know you have it. Now you're going to tell me where to find it."

"Look, I don't know who you are and I don't know what you think I have. I'm just a tourist. I was here for the long weekend. Then I go back home where I'm just a church secretary. You must have me mistaken for somebody else."

He grabbed the blindfold and yanked it up off of her head. She blinked in shock as she found herself staring at a guy who looked like a younger version of Uncle. He was holding up a picture of her. It was blurry, but there she was at Pearl Harbor.

"You want to tell me I've made a mistake and this isn't you?" he asked.

"I don't understand. Yes, that's me. I visited the memorial. So?"

"So, you're going to tell me everything you know."

"I don't know anything!" Tears of frustration and fear burned her eyes.

A creak above their heads caused him to look up with a scowl. He turned and climbed up a narrow set of stairs and slammed the door at the top closed behind him.

Cindy scooted forward to the edge of her chair and then off it and onto her knees with a thud. She bit back a yelp of pain as her left knee landed on something sharp.

She could hear voices but didn't stop to focus on hearing what was being said. She rolled onto her back and doubled her knees up. She pushed off the floor with shoulders and feet, arching her back.

Her hands were handcuffed behind her back. If she could get them in front of her she could hopefully get her legs untied and find something she could use as a weapon. She should have tried before but she'd still been too dazed to think clearly.

She struggled, trying to stretch her arms far enough that she could get her wrists under her rear. She arched her back harder until it felt like she was going to break her spine and she strained harder. Her hands were getting coated in blood from where the metal was digging into her wrists.

Finally she made it and then strained to make it past her legs. The voices upstairs were getting louder and she contorted herself as much as she could. She needed just another inch of clearance.

Her right ankle twisted painfully as she forced her hands around the feet. Finally she cleared them and she had her hands in front of her. She sat up and began to work at the knot on the rope binding her legs. Her hands slipped and she wiped them on the dress.

Geanie will never let me borrow anything else. Even as she struggled to undo the knots she couldn't believe how the absurdest things could come to mind even when your life was in danger.

A fingernail snapped off and another bent backwards. She kept going and finally the knot began to give. She redoubled her efforts as she could hear more footsteps above her. The knot was loosening ever so slowly and she wanted to scream. Finally, it came free, and she yanked the rope off her legs and stood up.

Her right ankle twisted underneath her but she caught herself on the chair before she could fall. Even though the boat was docked she could still feel motion and it made her that much more unsteady on her feet. She turned and made her way limping to the door as quickly as she could. She took the stairs, using her hands to support much of the weight on her right side which was hard given the handcuffs.

She held her breath as she pushed at the door. It was unlocked. She knew she'd have only a minute to run for it. She didn't know which part of the boat she was in or where the men were. If she tried to make it to the dock someone might see her and help her, but that would depend on where they were. She knew that some parts of the island were very isolated. They might not even be on the same island. If she made it into the water it would be a simple thing for them to catch her.

With her hurt ankle and wrists still cuffed together she couldn't trust to speed. So she'd have to rely on stealth. She opened the door just enough so that she could see out. She was facing the ocean and couldn't see anything but water.

The voices were coming through clearly now. Money seemed to be the topic of conversation. Maybe if she was very lucky the two men would kill each other. She eased the door open and slipped out, half crouching. She closed the door quietly. There was a wall behind her with the door in the center of it. She eased her way to the one side of it and peeked around the corner.

She could see the two men talking heatedly.

She pulled back and moved to the other side of the boat. She peeked around the wall there and couldn't see anyone. In front of her the railing was only about three feet tall. If she could get over the side and into the water without getting caught maybe she could make it to another boat.

She scurried to the railing and hoisted her left leg over, noticing that her knee was bloody. She turned and saw that there were little drops of blood to show where she'd gone. She didn't have time to worry about it, though. A round life preserver was hanging on the railing and she grabbed it and put it over her head. Handcuffed it would be hard to swim effectively and quietly. The preserver, as long as there was nothing wrong with it, would make her job easier.

She eased her right leg over the railing and nearly froze as she looked down at the ocean beneath her. It was a good four foot drop into the water from the lowest part of the rail. She eased herself down as low to the water as she could and then finally lowered herself down. Her feet and calves went into the water and then it was time to let go.

Terror surged through her. She didn't want to fall into the water. She didn't want them to hear her do so either.

God, please help me, she prayed. She let go, grabbing the life preserver as she did. She dropped into the water with enough force to almost tear the life preserver out of her hands. She clung to it, though, gritting her teeth at how much noise she had just made. At least she was on the opposite side of the boat. Plus the two men were arguing so loudly hopefully they didn't hear her splash.

She positioned the life preserver just in front of her so it was keeping her head and part of her chest out of the water. Then she began to kick, making sure to keep her legs underwater to minimize the sound. She knew instantly it was going to be hard going. She kicked off her sandals, wondering why she hadn't thought to do so earlier.

You can do this, she told herself. *Just keep kicking.*

Behind her she heard a gunshot ring out and her heart jumped. One of the men must have shot the other. Maybe she was safe.

More likely, though, her escape was about to be discovered. She gave up all pretense at stealth as she kicked wildly, heading for the next boat over at the dock. Her knee was stinging like fire from the salt water and her ankle was throbbing with every kick.

She was halfway between the two boats. She was going to make it. Once on board hopefully she'd be able to call for help. How long would it take the authorities to arrive? Could she hide long enough to be safe?

Something hit the water inches from her and a moment later she heard another gunshot.

He's shooting at me, she realized. She tried to change course, to zig zag, but she was moving impossibly slow. Water splashed her in the face and she coughed on it, choking. She couldn't breathe and the pain was becoming unbearable. She saw someone on the other boat and she tried to shout but just sucked in more water. She couldn't wave her arms without abandoning her life preserver and her injured legs wouldn't allow her to tread water for very long. If she tried to float she'd just be a sitting target.

She had to keep going. She kicked as hard as she could, until the pain was nearly blinding. Another bullet went into the water nearby. Then another splashed water into her eyes.

She didn't dare risk looking behind her. She just tried to focus on her destination. It was a small yacht with the name *Pearl of the Deep* written on it.

Her life preserver jerked, and she saw a

bullet hole in it just as she heard the shot ring out.

She swerved again, wishing she knew how many bullets before the man would have to reload. At the rate they were going it seemed that he would run out of bullets before she could reach the other ship.

Finally the *Pearl of the Deep* loomed in front of her. She aimed for a ladder on the side. She reached it and hauled herself out, praying she didn't get shot as she did so. She made it onto the boat and collapsed on the deck. She was dizzy and sick with exhaustion.

A shadow fell over her and she glanced up to see a man looking at her in surprise. He was wearing khaki shorts and a salmon colored polo shirt and looked to be in his forties. He was staring at her with open curiosity.

"Where did you come from?" he asked.

"Please help me," she sobbed. "I've been kidnapped. And now they're trying to kill me! It's that boat over there," she said, pointing. "They were shooting at me."

"That's one of the worst things I've ever heard," he said, shaking his head.

"Please, can you call the police?" she begged. "And get down. They might shoot you, too."

"If they couldn't hit you when you were ten feet away I'm sure they won't be able to hit me now," he said, smiling.

He doesn't believe me, she realized in despair. *How had he missed hearing the gunshots?*

"Please, you don't understand. We're in terrible danger," she sobbed. "Call Kapono. He's a detective with the Honolulu police. He'll be able to help."

"Not in time, my dear," the man said, crouching down beside her. "I'm afraid you're a long way from Honolulu."

She heard shouting and she twisted her head around so she could finally see the dock. The guy she recognized as her kidnapper was running down it.

"Please we have no time!" she insisted, struggling to get up. "That man on the dock is the one who kidnapped me."

"But what does he want with you?" the man asked.

"I don't know! He thinks I have something."

"Maybe you should just give it to him."

"I would, but he won't even tell me what it is. How can I give him something when I have no idea what it is he wants?"

The man shook his head. "That is a conundrum. Well, you know what they say?"

"What?" she asked as she made it to her feet.

"You just can't get good help these days."

7

Tuesday morning Jeremiah was waiting in his office when Mark arrived for his first official counseling appointment. He had spent the last couple of hours prepping himself mentally for the challenge ahead. When the detective entered his office Jeremiah was able to greet him with a smile that was relaxed and confident.

"Good morning," he said.

Mark grunted. "Not from where I'm sitting."

Jeremiah clasped his hands together. "You know when it comes to these sorts of things a lot is dependent on your attitude."

"Then we're in for a world of hurt," Mark admitted.

"So, I noticed."

Jeremiah leaned back in his chair. "Let's get started."

"Okay, what do you want me to do?"

"For now, I'd just like you to talk about

whatever's on your mind."

"Well, baseball season is upon us."

Jeremiah recognized a stalling tactic when he heard one. It was no matter. If Mark didn't want to jump right in he had ways of getting him to open up.

"Yeah, what team do you cheer for?

"Dodgers."

Jeremiah nodded. "I find it fascinating that baseball is America's past time when it seems like football is America's passion."

"It's like comparing apples and oranges. Two entirely different things and two entirely different experiences."

"Oh?" Jeremiah asked politely.

"Sure, football is how tough and gritty the fighting gets. You ever go to a baseball game though?"

"I haven't," Jeremiah said.

"Whole different feel. It's like going to a backyard barbeque. Everyone's just there soaking up the sun, enjoying the company, and watching some guys play. Doesn't matter who you are, where you come from, everyone's welcome."

"Is that so?" Jeremiah asked.

"Yeah. In June every year Paul and I would go catch a game. For a couple of hours there was no work, no bad guys to catch, just a couple of guys hanging out. I looked forward to that game every year."

"And this year?"

Mark's face clouded over. "Got the tickets a while back, but I don't have anyone to go with. It's a shame, too. We always had a good time."

"And now you can't because he's dead."

"Yeah. And part of me is pissed at him for that," Mark said.

"He bailed on one of the most special events of the year for you. It's understandable that you're angry."

"Yeah. Imagine that. I'm furious with him for getting himself killed."

There was a moment of silence as Jeremiah allowed Mark to process what he'd just said.

"Stupid, huh?" Mark said after a minute.

"The death of someone we care about often feels like a betrayal even though our rational mind knows they didn't want to leave."

Mark nodded. "Yeah, but Paul really mucked it up good. He didn't just die. I mean, a hundred times one or both of us could have gotten killed while we worked cases, arresting killers. He couldn't just take a bullet that way and make it easier on everyone. No, he got himself killed after he stuck me with a mess. He knew what I'd do to that guy in the interrogation room. He made sure I would, pushed my buttons right before he left. And, then, on top of all of that, I find out he was lying to me every day. I had to find out from the coroner that I didn't know the first thing about who my partner, my best friend, really was."

Jeremiah could see the pain and the anger burning inside Mark. They had touched on some of the core problems he needed to deal with. They had gotten there even faster than he would have imagined.

"What was he lying about?" Jeremiah asked.

Mark hunched his shoulders and locked his jaw as he averted his eyes. "He was lying about who he was. Turns out the real Paul got killed as a kid and the one I knew took that kid's place."

"A changeling?" Jeremiah asked, trying to mask the sudden interest he felt.

"I guess. The family won't talk to me about it. They found bones in that mass grave up at the camp that belong to the real Paul. You'd think his family would want answers just as much as I do."

"Maybe not. Any way you look at it, their son and brother is dead. Figuring out whether he died as a kid or a couple of months ago won't bring either the real Paul

or the imposter back and will just compli-
cate their lives and the grieving process
needlessly."

"Sometimes you make a lot of sense,"
Mark said.

Jeremiah shrugged noncommittally.

"Anyway, nobody wants to deal with it.
Seems I'm the only one who cares."

"You were his partner."

"Yes, yes I was."

Mark looked down at his hands and
Jeremiah could sense the grief that was
pouring through him.

Mark cleared his throat and when he
spoke again his voice sounded ragged. "I
need to know. I trusted that man with my
life for years. I need to know the truth about
him."

"It's possible he didn't even know the full
truth. It's also possible he kept you in the
dark to protect you."

"That's not what partners, friends, do.
They tell each other their problems and
then work them out together."

And just like that the specter of his own
past and the fears that he had about Cindy
discovering his secrets reared its head. As
calmly as he could Jeremiah pushed the
thoughts to the side, reminding himself to
focus on Mark.

"Okay, so what can you do about how you feel?" Jeremiah prompted.

"I can find out the truth. Maybe that will help me find some peace with his death."

"And if you never find the truth?" Jeremiah asked.

The detective's face contorted. "I can't accept that. I have to find out the truth. I'm a detective. How can I expect to be a detective and do the job if I can't even find out the truth about my partner?"

"You're worried that the fact that you trusted him, never suspected that he wasn't who he said he was, means you're a bad detective?"

"Yes. I mean, no. I don't know."

"Is it possible for any detective to be right all the time?" Jeremiah asked.

Mark snorted. "Of course not. We're only human and we can only draw conclusions based on the evidence we have and what our experience tells us about that evidence."

"Okay. Did Paul ever give you any reason to suspect that he wasn't who he said he was?"

There was a pause so long Jeremiah began to think Mark wasn't going to answer at all. When he finally did, his voice was barely a whisper. "I've laid awake nights, going over everything. Every case, every conversation, anything I can remember about him trying to answer that very question."

Jeremiah waited a few moments before pushing. "And in all of your searching have you remembered anything that should have given you pause?"

Mark shook his head. "No, not one single cursed thing."

"Given the time spent together, the content of your conversations, would you expect that any detective could have found something suspicious?"

"No."

"Then why do you think you should have been able to do what no other detective could have?"

Mark took a shaky breath. "Because I'm beating myself up about something I had no control over."

Jeremiah didn't offer a comment, just sat and waited.

"So, are you saying I should just let it go?" Mark asked.

"What do you think?"

"I need to know the truth."

"I'm not suggesting you stop looking for it."

"Then I guess the point is, I have to let my guilt over not figuring out there was something wrong about him go."

"If you did, it would probably be a tremendous relief to you."

"Yeah, and to Traci," Mark said. "She's told me a hundred times that it wasn't my fault, that I couldn't have known. Why didn't I believe her?"

"Because you weren't ready to hear the truth. And because you know she loves you and wouldn't want you to suffer."

"Whereas I know you have no problem seeing me suffer," Mark said.

"It's not that I want to see you suffer. I want you to heal. You can't heal unless you can first accept the truth about everything that happened . . . both good and bad."

Mark buried his face in his hands and shuddered. Jeremiah sat quietly. If Mark needed the space to scream or cry or laugh he'd give it to him. There were only so many human responses to grief or guilt or anger. He'd seen men go through all of them, sometimes in the span of a minute. Everyone coped in their own way but even then there were only so many ways of coping, or not coping, known to man. The important thing was to let Mark feel and express whatever emotions he needed to. The people that were ticking time bombs were the ones who didn't know how to express or had no safe forum to do so.

Ten minutes passed with Jeremiah hyper aware of each one. The counseling process was such a delicate one. With most, perhaps all, of the members of the synagogue he would have walked over and put a hand on their shoulder. Human touch was a powerful thing that could reach people when nothing else could.

Mark was a fighter though, a warrior despite the fact that he'd never been part of any army. He would need the human contact eventually, but he had to be ready to receive it. Trying to push him before he was ready to be that vulnerable would destroy everything they needed to achieve.

Finally Mark looked up. His eyes were moist but his cheeks were dry. "Thank you," he whispered.

"I only held the mirror, you were the one who saw the truth," Jeremiah said.

Mark stood abruptly. "I think I'm going to go for a walk. I need to think for a while."

Jeremiah nodded. "I think that sounds like an excellent idea."

Mark nodded and left, closing the door behind him. Jeremiah slumped a bit in his seat. It was true, he'd just been holding up a mirror to allow Mark to behold the truth but the effort he'd had to expend to make sure that Mark didn't catch a glimpse of the real him had been overwhelming.

He took several deep breaths as he re-assured himself. *You did well. He suspects nothing about you.* Well, nothing new at least. Thank G-d for small miracles.

Fortunately he had no appointments later that day. When he went out for lunch he told Maria that when she scheduled Mark's appointments to make sure he was the only appointment for those days. There was no way he could handle counseling anyone else so soon after his sessions with Mark. She looked puzzled since he'd never made a request like that when dealing with anyone else, but she agreed.

He went home and took Captain for a walk to clear his head. The dog happily paced beside him, tongue lolling. He was more grateful for the creature's presence than he could express. He himself had been on the verge of becoming a ticking time bomb a few months before. He found, though, that the more time he spent with the dog the calmer he was. He tried not to think about the fact that the dog was the only one he could truly be himself with.

The rest of the day passed swiftly and finally it was time to pick up Cindy from the airport. He felt a growing excitement as he drove. He had missed talking to her while she was gone and couldn't wait to hear all about her trip. Hawaii was one of the few places he'd never been and he'd dearly love to see it someday. He figured they'd grab some dinner and she could tell him all about it.

He reached the airport and opted to park the car and meet Cindy inside at baggage claim. The thought of circling the airport with the assorted locals and tourists all racing to cut each other off was not his idea of a good time.

Besides, meeting someone at baggage claim was more personal, special. *Maybe a little too special,* his inner voice whispered. Where Cindy was concerned he'd been ignoring that voice a lot lately.

After parking his car he made it into the baggage claim area. People hurried here and there, some arriving on business or vacation and others returning home. He had always found airports fascinating. They were filled with people from every walk in life who only shared one common goal and that was to get somewhere. An older gentleman walked by him, leaning heavily on his cane. Jeremiah couldn't help but wonder if the man realized that the woman who brushed past him was a famous actress, one whose movies he almost assuredly had never seen.

Jeremiah couldn't help but chuckle. Airports were an amazing place to people watch. You could tell so much about people just by observing how they navigated through the spaces and handled the stresses of travel.

He found a monitor that listed the carousel for Cindy's flight and moved to stand by it. A few minutes later a steady stream of passengers began to fill the space around him, all anxious to find their luggage and leave.

The conveyor belt began to move and the thud-thud-thud of bags sliding down the chute and onto it started up. Jeremiah stepped a few feet farther away from it to allow more people to claim their bags. He kept eager watch for Cindy.

Finally the trickle of people coming his way seemed to stop.

She had probably been one of the last ones off the plane. She might have stopped in the restroom before heading to baggage claim. A couple more minutes passed and he began to feel anxious. He knew he couldn't have missed her. He also knew that the suitcase she'd had with her when she left was way too large for her to have tried to take it as a carry-on. She had to have checked it.

He pulled out his phone. No missed calls. He tried dialing her phone but it went directly to voicemail.

"Excuse me," he said to one of the women standing near him.

She turned and frowned at him suspiciously.

"I'm waiting to pick up my friend. I think I'm in the right place. We're you on flight 439 from Honolulu?"

"Yes. That's right. And there's my bag, so this is the right place," she said, before moving to retrieve a fuchsia roller bag.

I'm just being paranoid. There's a dozen reasons why she might be slow getting down here, he told himself.

He pulled his phone back out and called her home number. Her roommate, Geanie, answered.

"Hi, Geanie, it's Jeremiah."

"Hi! Did you pick up Cindy? Did she have a great time?"

"No, not yet. I'm waiting for her here in baggage claim and she hasn't shown up yet. She didn't tell you about any change of plans? She wasn't changing her flight or having someone else pick her up?"

"No. I haven't heard anything from her at all," Geanie said.

The warning bells were going off at full

volume in his head now. "Okay, if she calls tell her where I am."

"Sure. Call me when you find her."

He hung up and moved to a white courtesy telephone. A minute later the operator was paging Cindy all over the airport. His stomach twisted in knots as he waited. Finally he had to admit that she wasn't able to pick up the phone. He went to the service desk and found a plump, spectacled woman with a nametag that said Dorothy on it.

"Can I help you?" she asked.

"Yes. I'm picking up my friend and I can't find her. She's not answering her phone and I had her paged but no luck."

"Well, it can be a rather long walk."

He shook his head. "It looks like everyone else from her flight is here. I'm worried. Can you check and tell me if Cindy Preston made the flight? It was 439 from Honolulu."

"I'm sorry, sir, I can't release passenger information. I'm sure she'll give you a call soon. It's possible she missed her flight and she'll be here on the next one tomorrow morning."

He passed his hand through his hair, feeling his agitation grow. "If she missed her flight why didn't she call to let me know?"

"I'm sure I don't know, sir," the woman said, her smile slipping. He wanted to press but he could sense that she was about five seconds away from calling a security guard. He cursed under his breath. Ninety-nine percent of all the airport regulations and paranoia did nothing to stop terrorists, they just tormented everyone else.

He moved away from the help desk and took another scan of the area. He tried her phone again and again it went straight to voicemail. Finally, he called Mark.

"Hello?" the detective answered, sounding bone weary.

"Mark? I need your help. It's Jeremiah."

"I got that much from the caller id. What's going on?"

"I'm here at LAX. I'm supposed to pick up Cindy and I can't find her. She's not answering her phone and Geanie hasn't heard anything from her."

"Maybe her phone battery is dead and you two keep just missing each other."

"No, I've been waiting here in baggage claim. I would have seen her."

"Humor me and check outside to see if she's waiting on the curb for you to drive by."

Jeremiah ground his teeth but turned and strode out the nearest door. He looked up and down the sidewalk.

"No, she's not out here."

"Maybe she missed her flight. Maybe she had someone else pick her up."

"No!" Jeremiah said, simultaneously rejecting both proposals with more vehemence than he had intended.

There was a pause on the other end of the line. "Something I should know about?" Mark asked.

And even though the question infuriated him, Jeremiah couldn't help but notice that Mark must be doing better. He was getting his obnoxious sense of humor back.

"I'm supposed to pick her up. If she had missed her flight I'd think she would have called if she could have. I tried talking to someone at the airline but they refuse to tell me whether or not she actually got on board the plane."

"What do you want me to do?" Mark asked, sounding slightly bewildered.

"I want you to help me find her!" Jeremiah roared.

There was a pause. "Okay, I think you just need to take a deep breath and calm down. Cindy's a big girl. Maybe you got your wires crossed and it's the wrong day or she took a taxi."

Jeremiah closed his eyes and prayed for the patience not to kill someone. "Mark, I have a very bad feeling about this. Can you please find out if she was on that plane?"

"In case you've forgotten, I'm suspended. And if I get caught trying to play the cop card —"

"Ask someone else to do it. Surely someone at the department owes you a favor."

"You're serious about this," Mark said, starting to sound worried himself.

"When it comes to Cindy not being where she's supposed to be I'm always serious," Jeremiah said.

It was Mark's turn to swear. "You're right. Give me a couple of minutes and I'll call you back."

Jeremiah paced while he waited. The area around the carousel cleared out and there was no one left. One single black bag circled lonely and he double-checked to make sure it wasn't hers. Finally the conveyor belt stopped.

When his phone rang he practically shouted hello as he accepted the call. "Jeremiah," Mark said, his voice stressed. "I was able to verify that Cindy had a ticket for the flight but she never showed up. The airline doesn't have a record of her changing the ticket and no airlines have her leaving Hawaii on any other flights."

Jeremiah stood, mind racing. If she wasn't scheduled on another flight then it wasn't something so simple as her missing her flight.

"Hello? Can you hear me?" Mark asked. "Jeremiah?"

"I'm going to call her hotel. You start calling hospitals," Jeremiah said.

And for a wonder Mark didn't argue with him. Jeremiah pulled the piece of paper out of his pocket that had all Cindy's trip information on it. He found the hotel phone number and called it.

As it rang he realized that his hands were shaking. How many people from his past would be amazed to see that? He stared at his left hand. *I'm in shock,* he realized. He knew he was jumping to conclusions, that he should calm himself down.

But he couldn't. Because it was Cindy. And deep down in his gut he knew she was in trouble.

8

"No!" Cindy gasped as she realized the implications of what the yacht owner had just said. She spun and lunged for the railing. If she could make it back in the water she had a chance to escape.

An iron hand clamped down on her shoulder and yanked backward hard enough to sweep her off her feet. She landed on her back with enough force to jar every bone in her body and her teeth snapped together.

She needed to get back up but her head was spinning. When she looked up the man's face floated in her vision.

"I'm afraid, my dear, you're out of the frying pan and in the fire, so to speak. I gave that idiot orders to kill you after he recovered our property from you."

Belatedly she realized he was the shouting man she'd heard when she first came to in the hull of the other boat. She heard pounding feet and a minute later her kidnapper was standing over her as well.

"Sorry, Boss."

"What happened over there?" the other man demanded.

"Nothing. I took care of it."

"Like you took care of her? Not good enough. Tell me everything."

"That guy came out of nowhere. I don't know how he knew I was here. He thinks I owe him —"

The yacht owner raised a hand. "Spare me your tales of financial woe. Did you kill him?"

Her kidnapper nodded.

"Great, so you're going to have to clean that up, too."

"Don't worry about it, Boss, I can handle it."

"No, if you could handle it, it would already be handled. Now just shut up and stand there and don't shoot off your mouth or your gun until I tell you."

He turned to Cindy.

"You have posed more of a problem than I would have thought," he said, almost conversationally.

"Who are you?" Cindy asked, struggling to understand what was happening to her.

He smiled at her. "You can call me Mr. Black, and this," he said, indicating the other man, "is my associate."

"That sounds like a fake name," she blurted out, not knowing what else to say.

"It's as real a name as you're going to get, sweetheart. Now, let's talk about what you have and how you're going to give it to me."

"That's the problem, I have no idea what anyone's talking about."

"Okay, I'll play along, for a while. Uncle, you remember him?"

She blinked at him. "The dead restaurant owner?"

"Yes, that Uncle. Very good. See, I knew you were a smart girl. So, let's talk about Uncle."

"I found his body. I went to his restaurant for lunch and there was no one there and the cash register was open and it all just seemed weird. I went into the kitchen and found his body and then I called the police."

"Of course you did. Smart. Nice job posing as the innocent bystander by the way, couldn't have done better myself. Clever girl. Now be a clever girl and give me what I want."

"I wasn't posing!" she half-yelled, desperate to make him understand.

"Save it for someone who believes it. When you found Uncle dead, what did you do with it?"

"Do with what?" she asked, choking on a sob. This was stupid. Why wouldn't someone just tell her what they were looking for? She swallowed hard. Mr. Black had told the other guy to kill her when he got what he wanted. If they knew for sure she didn't have what they wanted wouldn't they go ahead and kill her anyway?

She struggled, trying to figure out what to do, what to say that wouldn't get her shot.

"Come on. It wasn't in your room. You clearly hid it somewhere. Just be a good girl and tell me where."

"Why should I if you're just going to kill me?" she asked, stalling for time to think.

And then she heard a siren in the distance. Police! They must have been called because someone heard the gunshots. Her heart leapt.

"This is what happens when you get sloppy," Mr. Black said, turning to glare at his associate. "Now, go clean up the mess on the other boat before they search it."

"But the girl —"

"Leave her to me," Mr. Black said. He ducked inside the cabin for a moment and then came back out with what looked like a pillowcase. She stared at him in shock, wondering what he intended to do with it. As he moved toward her head she understood. He meant to blindfold her. That meant that not only would she not be able to see where he was taking her but also that she wouldn't be able to watch to see what new dangers were coming her way.

The man who had kidnapped her leered at her, his eyes sullen. As Mr. Black moved the cloth close to her head she smelled something pungent.

"Please, don't blindfold me again. I'll be good."

"Oh, you won't be giving me any trouble."

He put the pillowcase over her head. She sucked in air to scream.

And her world went black again.

Jeremiah hung up. A woman at the front desk of the hotel Cindy was staying at had just informed him that she'd never checked out that day. He began moving, heading for the ticketing counters even as he called Marie.

"Hello?" his secretary answered.

"It's Jeremiah. I've got a bit of a . . . family emergency." He winced. He knew his secretary didn't like Cindy and didn't approve of the time he spent with her. He was in no mood for a lecture now.

"Is everything okay?" she asked, alarm clear in her voice.

"I don't know yet. I'm getting on a plane. Can you please take care of Captain for a couple of days? I've got a spare house key in my desk with the pens."

"Of course. What else can I do to help?"

"Cancel all my appointments for the rest of the week. I'm not sure how long I'll be."

"All right. The gentleman who's coming in to meet with you tomorrow hasn't given us any contact info, though."

Jeremiah shook his head. Otto wouldn't be happy, but there was nothing he could do about it at the moment.

"Then give him my apologies and get it from him. Try to reschedule him for next week. He's bringing something for me, if he leaves it just put it in my office."

"You've got it."

"Thanks."

He hung up just as he made it to a ticketing agent.

"I need to be in Honolulu as fast as possible," he told the woman.

"We've got a flight that leaves at 6:35 in the morning."

"Not good enough. I needed to be there already."

She frowned. "The only flight tonight leaves in twenty minutes. I don't think —"

"I'll take it." He slammed his driver's

license and his credit card down on the counter. "Please call the gate and tell them I'm coming. It's a family emergency."

"I'll see what I can do."

Two minutes later he was standing in the line for security, chafing at the delay. He watched in disgust as they signaled out a man with crutches for extra screening. The guy was well-dressed, traveling with his wife, and looked like he was ex-military. What the idiots of the TSA didn't realize was that whatever flight that guy was on would be one of the safest flights possible. A terrorist wouldn't survive three seconds with someone like him on the plane.

Or someone like me.

At last he made it out the other side. His gate was at the far end of the airport and the plane would be leaving it in five minutes. He ran. The airport was crowded and he had to dodge in and out, running around other startled travelers.

One woman dropped her bags in front of him and bent to pick them up. He had no choice and he vaulted over her. He would make that plane and no one could stop him.

At last he made it to the section of the airport he needed to be in. His gate was at the far end and he saw a lone flight attendant standing, waving him on. He put on a fresh burst of speed, relieved that this section was empty.

She moved over to stand in front of the door to the jetway and he flung his ticket at her, pausing only long enough for her to hand it back. He raced down and the flight attendants clustered inside the door of the plane parted way for him.

He heard them close the door behind him as he made his way to his seat. Fortunately it was on the aisle and he slid into it. As he buckled his seatbelt the plane backed away from the gate and he closed his eyes.

He could hear the flight attendant giving the safety spiel. He didn't bother paying attention. He'd heard it thousands of times before. And if the plane went down he already had his own safety plans well figured out years earlier.

The guy in the seat next to him was nervous. He could smell the fear on him. Jeremiah opened his eyes a crack and turned his head slightly to study his travel companion. The man had the white-knuckle look of a terrified flyer, not the nervous anticipation of a terrorist.

Reassured, Jeremiah closed his eyes again. He wondered where Cindy was and what she was going through. He should have never let her go on vacation alone.

But who am I to make those kinds of decisions about her life? he chided himself.

I'm no one, just a friend. It's not my place.

Though the thought made him inexplicably sad, he knew it was the truth. He tried to take comfort from that. It was not his right to stop Cindy from doing anything she pleased regardless of how dangerous it might be.

It was Hawaii. It shouldn't have been dangerous. In his gut, though, he knew that wasn't a real excuse. Pine Springs wasn't a dangerous place either. Still, Cindy always managed to seem to find trouble. Or it found her. Either way, trouble and she seemed to go together.

Even though it wasn't his job to save her, he knew that he would always feel compelled to. He knew that if he was going to save her now he needed to be alert and focused once he landed in Honolulu.

He slumped down in his seat and focused his breathing. Before the wheels were off the tarmac, he was asleep.

Mark was pacing in his office like a man gone insane. Something was wrong. Something had happened to Cindy. Every instinct he had told him that, but there was absolutely nothing he could do about it. Even if he wasn't in his current state of suspension he was a California cop not a Hawaii one.

If only he had eyes and ears on island, some way he could help out. Jeremiah was going to need help, that much he was certain of. The rabbi was incredibly resourceful and resilient but he was going into completely unknown territory and he was going blind.

Since he wouldn't be able to prove that Cindy was technically missing yet he'd get precious little help from the Honolulu police department either. And suddenly he stopped pacing. A friend he had gone to college with who had been from the islands and had gone into law enforcement as well. They barely spoke anymore, just sent the occasional Christmas cards and he got email with pictures of the guy's kids and sent appropriate responses pertaining to how big they were getting.

And a light dawned in his mind as he remembered the last Christmas card he'd gotten from the guy and the big news he'd had to share about his promotion. And he knew he had an ally in Hawaii that could help Jeremiah, or at least get the search for Cindy going. He reached for his phone.

Cindy woke with a start. She blinked, trying to get her eyes to focus. Her head was buzzing and her tongue felt swollen and thick.

I've been knocked out again, she realized. She remembered the odor inside the pillowcase. She wondered if she could expect any kind of long-term brain damage from it all. In the next moment she realized it was ridiculous to worry about that when she was facing imminent death.

She forced herself to breathe in and out slowly as she tried to bring herself fully awake. The process was slow and she hated the hazy feeling.

Her chin was touching her chest and she slowly raised her head. Shooting pain shot up her neck and her shoulders felt like they were on fire. She winced as she finally got her head upright. She felt like her neck and her entire spinal cord was kinked.

Slowly she became aware of the rest of her body. Her hands were throbbing and she looked down to see them clenched into fists. Her wrists were tied tightly to the sides of a metal chair. She slowly forced her fingers open and they tingled. Her legs and ankles were lashed to the bottom of the chair. Her feet were tingly and going numb like they were falling asleep. She tried to wiggle her toes but it did no good.

Nothing seemed to be broken. She rolled her neck gingerly, trying to get it to loosen up as she stretched and flexed her fingers.

Finally she took stock of her surroundings. She was in a light, airy room with windows on three sides. She could see trees outside of the windows in the light from the fading sun and realized that from the angle she was looking at them she had to be on a second floor.

She blinked several times, trying to grasp what she was looking at. She could see outside. She wasn't in a basement and there were no curtains or blinds on the windows. Maybe she could signal for help. As she craned her neck around to look out each window, though, she realized that wouldn't work.

There wasn't a house or road in sight in any direction. Mr. Black, or whoever had her now, clearly had no fear of anyone seeing her here. Outside she could see a great many trees. A few were palm trees but the majority were something else. Behind the trees a mountain rose up toward the sky. She could see the tiniest trickle of a waterfall down it, but no houses or signs of civilization. The mountains were visible out of all three windows.

The room was bare except for a television

set mounted high on the wall. The walls were otherwise smooth and cream colored. The floors were wood and looked new. The whole room looked new, like a house that had never been lived in.

The television was on although there was no sign of a remote control. It was showing a rerun of some old cop show.

If only the real cops were on their way to find her. She had to hope that they were and that they would get there before it was too late. Mr. Black had never had a chance to answer her question about why she should cooperate with him. Maybe it was just as well. She had a feeling that where he was concerned she was dead no matter what she did.

At the thought she could feel her pulse accelerate and she started to breathe faster.

Calm down, don't hyperventilate, she told herself.

After a couple of minutes she was able to bring her breathing under control. She looked outside and couldn't tell anything about her location from the trees and mountains she saw.

Next she strained her ears, listening for sounds of life in other parts of the house. It was impossible to hear anything but the blare of her own television, though.

"Where am I and where is everyone else?" she whispered.

She tested her bonds but there was zero give in them and after a few minutes she gave up. All she could do was sit and wait.

And pray.

She got busy doing that.

Jeremiah spent the plane ride sleeping. He had learned when he was young that one of the first rules of survival in an uncertain situation was to sleep when you could and eat when you could because you didn't know when you'd be able to do either again. He knew that once the plane touched down in Honolulu he would not rest until he had found Cindy.

He woke to hear the captain's announcement that they'd be arriving shortly and that local time was three hours earlier than Los Angeles time making it still Tuesday, though barely. A couple of minutes later they touched down and began to taxi. He turned on his phone. The only message was from Mark telling him he'd called every medical facility on the island with no luck and asking him to call when he knew anything.

He tried calling Cindy's cell one more time but it again went straight to voicemail. He didn't bother leaving a message. He pocketed the phone and quietly eased his seatbelt off. He was more convinced than ever that something was really wrong and that he didn't want to be trapped behind people gathering their endless piles of carryon luggage and shuffling off the plane.

The moment the plane stopped next to the gate he ejected out of his seat and was halfway down the aisle before anyone else could even get their seatbelt off. He shoved past a guy at the front who swore at him. Jeremiah didn't care. The niceties of civilized society meant little to him. They were the rules he played by when the world was looking but they were not his rules.

"Family emergency," he said to the flight attendant who was manning the door when she looked at him with narrowed eyes.

She nodded and as soon as she was able to swing the door open she stepped back so he could go through. He did so at a run. A wave of warm, humid, fragrant air hit him like a wall and he breathed deep as he ran. He hit the terminal and people scattered in front of him.

He ran, his mind racing steps ahead of him. He would have a taxi take him to Cindy's hotel where hopefully he would find her safe and sound, though he knew that wouldn't be the case. Then he'd get into her room and try to piece together what happened to her. It was possible she was sick or injured and unable to call for help. And what made his gut twist was that he knew that was a best case scenario.

He made it to the baggage claim area and headed straight for ground transportation. People were grouped around, most carrying leis, some looking for loved ones. Others were drivers carrying signs bearing the names of their passengers.

And suddenly Jeremiah stumbled to a halt, bewilderment rushing through him. A large man who looked nothing like a chauffeur was holding a sign that said Jeremiah Silverman.

9

It was pitch dark and Cindy kept waiting for Mr. Black to show with threats and, hopefully, with food. Her stomach was beginning to growl angrily and she tried to figure out how long it had been since dinner with Kapono. Thinking about it just made her hungrier.

That was okay. She'd rather go without food than have to face her captors. How long had she been a prisoner? Were the police looking for her yet? From there she moved to thoughts of her kidnappers.

Mr. Black and the first guy. She didn't know what had happened to either of them. She didn't even know who either of them were. Why had they kidnapped her and what was it they thought she had?

Maybe if she could figure that out she could figure a way out of this mess. Maybe she should lie and tell them she'd have to take them to the location where she'd hidden it. Whatever *it* was. What had they thought she was supposed to give to Uncle? And why had they thought she'd be the person with it.

She replayed every move she'd made since landing at the airport in her mind. How could anyone have mistaken her for anything other than the tourist she was? She'd gone to Pearl Harbor, gone to the luau, gone on a snorkeling tour, even if she hadn't gone in the water. It was a good thing she hadn't. If she had —

She stopped. The faulty life preserver. Was it possible that it hadn't been an accident? Was it possible that Al had known there was something wrong with it when he tried to give it to her and when he tried to keep it from Marge? But why? Why was he trying to hurt her? Did he think she had whatever it was as well? Had he planned to go through her stuff while she was dead or injured looking for it? If so, how was he connected to Mr. Black and her attacker?

She closed her eyes, trying to tune out the blare of the television so she could think better. Al hadn't seemed to know who she was when she first got on the boat. It had been after she reminded him that she'd seen him at the archaeological site that his mannerisms had changed slightly and he'd offered her the life preserver. But that made no sense. All she'd seen was him doing his job. Maybe someone had called him and told him to kill her once the ship left port.

She sighed. She had no idea whether he was connected to the others or if it was just a coincidence about the life preserver or even if there were two groups of people out to kill her.

After they get whatever it is they're after.

It was something they thought she or someone would be giving to Uncle. It was sad, but she couldn't even remember the restaurant owner's real name.

So, maybe she could figure out what it is they were looking for. It was possible it was something in the restaurant at the time she was there. If so, and they hadn't found it yet, it was probably in some police evidence locker.

But she was not about to share that information anytime soon. After all Mr. Black had told the other man to kill her after he got what he wanted. It didn't seem like it was in her best interest to tell him that the police had it.

She mentally reviewed her time in the restaurant, trying to remember everything she'd seen. Maybe it had something to do with the cell phone that had been sitting unattended on the counter. But if that was what they were looking for, wouldn't they have taken it when they killed Uncle?

Unless they didn't kill Uncle, but someone else did.

Uncle, who killed you and why? she thought, frustration mounting.

Kapono had hinted that Uncle might be laundering money through his business. Were these people partners of his or perhaps rivals? If so, were they looking for something related to money? It made sense, but she still didn't see how they thought she had anything to do with it.

She thought about the rest of her conversation with Kapono. He had been surprised that the taxi driver had sent her to Uncle's. Why had he? Did he really like the food and it was just an innocent piece of advice? Or was he somehow involved as well?

Her head began to pound. The television was blaring very loudly and the more tired she became the louder it seemed. Between it and the hunger and her desperation to figure things out her head was beginning to throb and the room was starting to spin.

Her stomach was rumbling louder and she felt incredibly nauseated. Night was falling. It had to have been at least a day since she was kidnapped. It could have even been two.

She felt herself starting to panic and that just made her head hurt more.

It's going to be okay, she told herself. If they hoped to get any information out of her they were going to have to come back soon and give her something to eat and drink. Once she had that then she would feel better, stronger, and she could work on escaping. She just had to hold out a little longer.

Jeremiah approached the man with the sign warily. The man was wearing jeans and a T-shirt. He was easily seven feet tall with a broad chest and heavily muscled arms. He was scowling.

"I'm Jeremiah Silverman. Who are you?"

"Kapono Robinson. I'm a detective with the Honolulu Police Department."

"What's happened?" Jeremiah asked sharply.

"You tell me. My captain got a call from a buddy of his in Los Angeles. Said someone needed to pick you up, that a woman was missing."

Mark calling in more favors, Jeremiah realized.

"Okay, let's go," Jeremiah said.

He fell into step with Kapono, matching

his stride. "Why did they send you?" he asked.

"I was talking to the captain when he got the call. When I heard that the missing woman was Cindy I volunteered. I wanted to go to her hotel but he sent me to get you first."

"You know, Cindy? How?" Jeremiah asked.

They walked outside and an unmarked car was parked at the curb, lights going in the window. They got in. Kapono flipped off the light and pulled away from the curb.

"She was a witness in a homicide case over the weekend."

"Of course she was," Jeremiah said with a groan.

"What do you mean?"

"Trouble has a way of finding Cindy. What happened?"

"A local restaurant owner was murdered in his kitchen. She was the one who found the body and called 911."

Jeremiah leaned his head against the backrest and gritted his teeth. *Cindy, why didn't you call me?*

"Ultimately she didn't see anything, we didn't need anything else from her. Not really."

Jeremiah could tell by the hesitation in

the detective's voice that he wasn't telling the whole story.

"I just hope she's alright," Jeremiah said.

"She was fine when I dropped her off Sunday night," Kapono said.

"From where?"

There was a long pause. Too long. Jeremiah turned and looked at him. "Where were you coming from?"

Kapono wouldn't look at him; he just kept his eyes fixed on the road. "So, most people would call the police if they thought something had happened to someone. They wouldn't jump on the first plane they could and fly out here. Are you the boyfriend or something?"

"No, nothing like that," Jeremiah said.

"Are you sure?"

"Yes. Why, did she mention me?"

"No."

Jeremiah was surprised at the conflicting feelings that brought. Mostly he felt relief but it was tinged with something else. It felt like jealousy. He squashed it down. No time for complications like that.

"You took her out to dinner and then brought her back to her hotel Sunday night?" he guessed.

"Yes."

A retort about that not being very professional came to his lips but he bit it back. All he knew was that Cindy needed to stop going to dinner with guys, it got her into trouble.

More like I don't want her to go to dinner with other guys, he thought, frustrated with himself.

"How soon until we get there?" he asked.

"Ten minutes. We're lucky, very little traffic this time of night."

"Good."

"You know. Lots of people extend their vacations on a whim here. We're probably going to find out that's what's going on. It will be a big waste of your time and mine."

"Time well wasted to find out that's all it is," Jeremiah said.

"Why you don't think so?" he asked.

"It's not like her. Plus, she didn't change her plane reservation."

Jeremiah noticed that a moment later they were barreling down the road even faster. He didn't say anything and the two settled into silence. Jeremiah struggled not to count the minutes. He needed to clear his head. If Cindy was in trouble she would need him to be able to perform at his best.

By the time they parked at her hotel he had achieved mastery over himself. One way or another he would have answers shortly and until then there was nothing he could do but wait and prepare.

They took the escalator up to the lobby and approached the front desk.

"Aloha. Can I help you?" the lady behind the counter said.

Kapono pulled out his badge. "We need to know if Cindy Preston has checked out."

"Let me look that up for you," she said, eyes widening slightly. She typed the name into her computer. "No. She was scheduled to check out this morning, but she hasn't yet."

"We're going to need a key to the room," Kapono said.

"Of course," she said, hastily moving to make them a keycard. She handed it to Kapono seconds later. "Is there anything else?" she asked.

"Not now."

They moved to the elevator and once inside Jeremiah watched as Kapono rocked back and forth from foot to foot. He was getting anxious.

The hallway looked like any other. There was no one else around. They found her door and opened it. Kapono flicked on the lights. "Cindy?" he called.

There was no answer and he stepped over the threshold, posture tense. Jeremiah followed. Once inside Jeremiah stopped abruptly.

The place had been ransacked. The contents of her suitcase were spilled all over the room and the bag itself tossed in a corner.

"Wow, I didn't think she'd be so messy," the detective commented.

"Cindy didn't do this," Jeremiah growled.

"You seem pretty sure of that."

"Very sure," he said. He stepped all the way into the room and looked around. He wouldn't touch anything but he needed to get an idea of what had happened. "Someone was looking for something."

Kapono pulled a pair of gloves out of his pocket. "We're sure she didn't do this?"

"I'd stake my life on it. And I think whoever did this took her."

Kapono looked at him sharply. "What makes you think that?"

"Besides the fact that she's not back home right now? Her purse is here," Jeremiah said, pointing to the corner. There, crumpled underneath a standing lamp was Cindy's purse. They moved over to it. It's contents had also been dumped on the floor.

Kapono picked up the cell phone and depressed the button. "Battery's dead," he said.

He put it down and looked at the rest.

"Driver's license, credit cards."

"Look at the purse," Jeremiah said.

Kapono picked it up. The purse had been slashed, the lining cut out. The detective whistled. "I think you're right about one thing. Someone was definitely looking for something."

Jeremiah walked slowly around the room, eyes roving over everything. Cindy's royal blue shirt that he loved was crumpled on the floor by the closet next to her tennis shoes which had had the inner lining removed from them as well.

Then his eyes spotted a reflection off something shiny that was partway under the bed. "Over here," he called.

Kapono joined him and he pointed. The detective bent down and retrieved a rectangle of plastic and held it up.

"Her room key," Jeremiah said.

Kapono pulled out his cell phone. "I have to call this in, get a team out here to go over everything."

"Look," Jeremiah said, crouching down and pointing to a scrap of fabric on the floor about two feet from where the key had been. "I'd be willing to bet you're going to find something like chloroform on that."

"Oh man," Kapono said, running a hand through his hair.

Jeremiah stood slowly. "I'm right."

"I can't argue with you. I think she's been kidnapped."

Cindy tried desperately to sleep. Every time she closed her eyes, though, all she could hear was the blare of the television which had become like a drum beat thrumming in her head.

They're trying to drive me crazy with the sound, she thought. Sleep deprivation could make a person say things they shouldn't and they were probably hoping to use that against her.

Suddenly a new thought hit her. What if something had happened to Mr. Black? What if he had been arrested or killed? What if he was unable or unwilling to tell anyone where she was? She could starve to death waiting for help to come.

She screamed at the top of her lungs for help, praying that someone, somewhere would hear her. She kept it up for five minutes until her voice gave out. Her throat was raw and parched.

Maybe someone heard me. *Maybe they'll call the police.*

She dropped her head toward her chest praying for rescue.

■ ■ ■ ■

To their credit the police responded quickly to Kapono's call. Once the crime scene investigators arrived Kapono barred Jeremiah from the room. That was okay. They were unlikely to find anything new. Still, he had to school himself in patience as Kapono refused to let him leave the area. Finally the detective emerged from the hotel room and grabbed his arm.

"Let's go get some coffee and talk."

He had known this was coming and he had been preparing himself for it. He knew that in a kidnapping the first 48 hours were crucial, but he had to operate under the assumption that she had been taken immediately after returning to her hotel from dinner with the detective. That meant that they were already well past the 48 hour mark.

At this point all he had to go on was whatever he could glean from the detective about the murder that Cindy had stumbled upon. Ten minutes later they were sitting down at a table in Zippy's.

Knowing it would be a long conversation and a very long time before the opportunity to eat presented itself again, Jeremiah went ahead and ordered the teriyaki steak and a bowl of chili. The waitress gave him a huge grin and told him they were famous for their chili. He didn't care. He just knew that it would stick with him for a while and it might be a long time before he ate again.

"Okay. Now, I need you to help me out here," Kapono said as soon as the waitress had left. "Who would have wanted to hurt her?"

"Tell me who killed your restaurant owner and I'll tell you where to start looking," Jeremiah said.

Kapono shook his head. "There's nothing there, I told you. She didn't see anything. She just found the body."

"And we'll have a lot better chance of finding her still alive if you stop lying to me," Jeremiah said, pinning the other with his stare.

"I'm not lying to you."

"Well you're sure not telling me everything."

The man sitting across from him was nearly a foot taller and half a foot wider than him, and was not used to being challenged. Jeremiah had dealt with men that were far more intimidating than the detective, though. He knew how to dominate and he didn't have time to talk the other man around to his way of thinking.

So he looked him straight in the eyes and let the tiger out of the cage. He let the mask of civility slip, for just a moment, and let Kapono have one brief glimpse of the real him. It was the him that no one back home had ever seen. Not Mark, not Cindy.

Kapono responded on almost a visceral level to what he had seen, moving farther away from Jeremiah. The big man blinked rapidly as his conscious mind struggled to find words to explain what his subconscious mind had instantly understood.

"Listen to me very carefully," Jeremiah said, dropping his voice so soft that the other would have to strain to hear him. "I will find Cindy. Nothing, *no one,* will stand in the way of that."

Kapono nodded though he probably didn't even realize it.

"Good. Now, let's get to work."

Kapono nodded again, thought quickening in his eyes.

Jeremiah leaned back in his seat. "Tell me everything," he said, bringing his voice back to a conversational volume.

Kapono cleared his throat. "I'm sorry. I didn't know she was your girl."

Jeremiah didn't say anything. Better to let him think whatever he needed to in order to get the required results.

An hour later he had eaten his fill and had gotten every last bit of information that Kapono had, even some details the detective probably hadn't realized were important. Jeremiah took it all in, mind working to connect clues, to see everything. He knew every move Cindy had made that Kapono knew about.

After a promise to be in touch after he had more information, Kapono dropped Jeremiah back at Cindy's hotel where the rabbi was able to get a room. He needed a base of operations if nothing else. As soon as he stepped foot in his room his phone rang.

It was Mark. He answered.

"Thanks a lot for the babysitter," he growled.

"Hey, last thing I needed was for you to disappear over there and then I wouldn't know where either of you were."

Jeremiah didn't bother to acknowledge that.

"So, anything?" Mark asked, voice tense.

"Police have officially declared it a kidnapping."

He heard Mark suck in his breath. "Any leads?" "

"A few. It's not a lot to go on. Apparently

on Saturday she found a murder victim and called it in."

"Of course she did," Mark said.

"I know. Anyway, the police are tracking down their leads."

"What are you going to do?"

Jeremiah hesitated. His first instinct was to lie to Mark. The truth was, though, they'd been through some harrowing experiences together and Mark had already bent the rules just to help Jeremiah figure out what had happened to Cindy.

"You don't want to tell me, do you?" Mark asked quietly.

Jeremiah took a deep breath. "Not particularly."

"Look. We've never talked about what happened up at Green Pastures, when you were on that mountain with the kids. But somehow you got them all out safe even with assassins after you. Clearly you have . . . skills. I don't know where they come from and frankly I don't want to know. What I do want to know is whether there's anything I can do to help."

"I'll let you know if something comes up."

"Fair enough. And promise me one thing?"

"What?"

"Be careful. I really don't want to have to

go back to the department shrink."

Jeremiah hung up. He wasn't about to make promises like that. Not when there was dark work to be done. Not when Cindy's life hung in the balance.

He closed his eyes and pictured her face in his mind.

Hold on, Cindy, I'm coming for you.

10

"Is everything okay?" Traci asked, yawning as she came into the room.

Mark sat staring at his cell phone. "No, it's not," he said finally.

"What's wrong?" she asked.

He didn't want to tell her, but she deserved to know the truth. He looked up. "Cindy's been kidnapped."

All the color drained from Traci's face and she clutched her robe more tightly around her as she sat down on the couch next to him. "Are you sure?" she asked.

He hated the way her hands were starting to shake. He reached out and grabbed her free hand. It had been only half a year since Traci had been kidnapped. It had only been for a few hours but it had been the most terrifying hours of both of their lives. And Cindy had helped save her.

"I'm afraid so. She was on vacation in Honolulu. Jeremiah's flown over there to help find her."

"What has she gotten herself into now?" Traci burst out, voice thick with distress.

"Another murder, it sounds like."

"Why can't she leave these things to the police? She's going to get hurt."

Mark squeezed her hand. He had felt the same way so many times in the past. But if Cindy never got involved, Traci might be dead. A lot more people, too.

"I don't mean that," Traci said, hurriedly, as if remembering herself. "I just hope she's okay."

"Me, too."

"Do you need to go over there?" she asked.

He shook his head slowly. "I'd just get in the H.P.D.'s way. Jeremiah's too, for that matter. Besides, I'm sure my bosses wouldn't approve."

"But she's your friend. They both are."

He was about to deny it, but then he had to stop and reflect for a moment. Cindy and Jeremiah had started out as citizens in need of his help, his protection. They had quickly graduated to pains in his posterior that needed protecting from themselves. He had grudgingly admitted at last that they were concerned citizens with incredible instincts and a penchant for finding trouble. At some point in there had they become friends? They must have. Otherwise, how else could he explain his behavior two months earlier?

"The last time I thought of them, treated them as friends, I ended up torturing a suspect and nearly destroying us," he whispered. It was still so hard to admit, to discuss, even with Traci who had been there with them, who had helped save him when he didn't think he was worth saving.

It was her turn to squeeze his hand. "Whatever you need to do, I'll support you."

That was his Traci. Always there for him, his rock. He pulled her close and held her until they both fell asleep there on the couch.

After hanging up with Mark Jeremiah left his room and made his way up to the next floor. The door to Cindy's room was barricaded with yellow police tape. Once he had used the keycard he had lifted off of Kapono he ducked under the tape and entered the room, quickly closing the door behind him. The police had been thorough, but he needed to examine everything for himself.

The detective had said that when he and Cindy were out to dinner she had been wearing a black dress and sandals. He quickly searched through the closet and the drawers and discovered a nightgown but no dress. He also found a pair of tennis shoes but there was no sight of the sandals either.

Which confirmed the suspicions he'd had earlier when he'd seen the room key partially under the bed. She had been grabbed pretty soon after she got back to her room before she had a chance to change. Most likely it had been immediate since she hadn't had a chance to put the room key away. That helped. It meant she had for sure been taken that night as opposed to later in the evening after going to a store or in the morning returning from breakfast.

Whoever had kidnapped her had been waiting in her room while she was at dinner with the detective. Although it was possible someone had seen them together at dinner and kidnapped her in some sort of revenge scheme against Kapono it was unlikely. No clear message had been sent to him and the kidnappers would have already had to know which hotel she was staying at.

He had already dismissed Kapono as not being involved. The man was an honest cop and his concern for Cindy was genuine. He couldn't have hidden either of those things from Jeremiah. He had always been able to read people incredibly well.

Ironically it was a skill he had worked hard to suppress once he had come to America and became a rabbi. Ordinary people lied all the time, everything from the polite, white lies about things as mundane as whether a dress made someone look fat to the big, life shattering lies. They lied to themselves every day. They lied to him because they didn't want him to know what they'd been doing on the Sabbath instead of reflecting on G-d. They also lied to him in therapy which was the saddest of all because only the truth could set them free.

So, he worked hard to ignore the lies and the half-truths that people in polite society told so that everything would remain nice and neat and polite in their little worlds. When he wanted to, though, the ability was still there, just a thought away. He had to be ever vigilant about using it at inappropriate times but when he needed it, he could count on it.

That was how he knew Kapono was telling him everything he knew. He grabbed a pair of gloves out of his pocket. He had gotten them from a box Kapono kept in his car. It was important that he look through everything and he needed to do so without leaving evidence of his visit.

He found all the receipts that were scat-

171

tered around the room. He studied each of them carefully, memorizing where she'd gone and the order in which she'd gone to them. The night of her arrival she'd had breakfast in the hotel. Unless her kidnappers were other hotel guests it didn't make sense that there was any problem there.

And if her kidnappers had seen her at dinner or breakfast the next morning what could she possibly have done or said that would lead to her being kidnapped? No, the logical answer was that her kidnapping had something to do with the body she'd found in the restaurant.

The restaurant had been her second stop of the day. Kapono had told him that she had walked there from Pearl Harbor, a fact that surprised the detective. It would have made more sense for her to have taken a taxi off base. Cindy walking through a military base when it wouldn't have been normal for a person to do so was definitely something he should investigate, the first abnormal thing she had seemingly done since arriving in town.

He pieced it all together through the conversation with Kapono and the receipts that he rifled through. He should be able to recreate her Saturday and Sunday from Pearl Harbor up to the moment she was kidnapped.

Ideally he would have started in the morning after the sun was up and people were awake. He wanted to wait until the exact time of day that Cindy had done each thing, just to detect if there were any patterns or things that were time occurrences that she might have witnessed. He didn't want to wait that long, though, to get started.

He looked at the time stamp for the gift store at Pearl Harbor. He hoped someone there remembered her. It would help if he could get an idea of her moods and actions during the course of those days. Had Cindy found trouble other than the murdered restaurateur?

He picked up her camera and began to look at the photos. There were shockingly few on there and he started to think she might have taken pictures with her phone instead. He finally found the phone behind the curtains. Someone had smashed it and it wouldn't turn on. He debated about putting it back. It looked like the police had missed it in their search, but he was loathe to risk removing something they might notice.

He shook his head. If they had found it, they would have taken it with them as evidence and tried to find a way to get the data off of it. He slipped the phone in his pocket and returned to the search.

Cindy was exhausted and hungry. She had no idea how long she had been awake or even what day it was. She was sitting, tied to a chair, and had been for so long that she'd long ago lost the feeling in her bottom and her feet. She tried to shift but nothing seemed to work.

Every time she felt like she was going to finally drift off and get some sleep a commercial would come on, loud and blaring, and jolt her awake. The muscles in her eyelids spasmed and she gritted her teeth, hating the sensation. She was so tired she could feel her own pulse pounding through her body. It wasn't fast necessarily but she was hyper aware of it.

Her terror had given away to a dull, mind-numbing feeling of fear mixed with misery. She had given up trying to figure out what her captor was going to do to her. She was actually starting to think he might let her starve to death or go out of her mind with exhaustion.

A news show came on. Apparently it was six in the morning. She swung her head toward one of the windows, but it was still dark outside. She turned back, staring blankly at the television screen, processing very little of what was crossing it.

A picture of a woman flashed up and with a start she realized it was her. Fully alert she listened to the rest of the announcement. The police knew that she was missing. They were searching for her.

Despair filled her. She wasn't missing, she was kidnapped. Until they got that straight they'd be looking in all the wrong places, like the ocean and hiking trails and places where a tourist could get lost or injured. Tears stung her eyes. Had they gone through her room? Why hadn't they figured out she had been kidnapped?

She wondered if Kapono was worried and in the next breath she realized that the police had probably called her home. Geanie would have answered the phone, been told that she was missing. Geanie would have called Jeremiah to tell him.

Jeremiah.

She had to get free. She had to see him again. If he could survive assassins trying to kill him and a bunch of teenagers in the woods then she could survive this. She looked around. If only she could find a way to signal to someone, to let them know that she was here and alive and *kidnapped.*

A sudden sound in the hallway caused

every muscle in her body to tense so suddenly that half of them cramped. She bit her lip and struggled not to cry out with the pain of it all.

I'm dehydrated, she realized as the muscles in her left hand continued to spasm before the fingers curled into the palm like claws and stayed there. The pain was excruciating and even worse was the desperate sensation of *wrongness.*

An image darkened the doorway and then the overhead light flicked on. Mr. Black was standing, arms crossed, staring at her. She tried to read his expression but his face was neutral. He stared at her for what seemed like an impossibly long time, as though he was trying to make his mind up about something. Finally, he gestured to the television.

"Someone *finally* realized you were missing," he said.

She heard the emphasis he put on the word *finally.* He wanted her to think that it was unusual that it had taken so long, that no one cared, that she was unimportant. But she wouldn't let him do that to her.

"They'll come for me," she said. She tried to put as much conviction into her voice as she could. Maybe if he thought people were searching for her, he'd let her go. She knew it was a long shot, but she had to try.

He smiled that slow, creepy smile that made her skin crawl. "I very much doubt that. Oh, I'm sure they'll look for you. But they'll never find you. They'll spend a few days combing Honolulu and then the rest of the island before they give up."

"They might find me," she said, hoping she sounded defiant.

"No, they won't. You're not on Oahu."

He might as well have slapped her. She could feel herself reeling from the impact of the revelation. Her worst fears had been realized. She had left the island completely and they wouldn't know to look for her on a different island.

"Where, where am I?" she asked at last.

"One of the other islands," he said with a shrug.

"I kind of figured that out on my own," she said, struggling to keep the sarcasm out of her voice. She reminded herself that she didn't know how he would respond if provoked.

"Good. Then I'll leave it for you to figure out which island," he said with a smug smile.

Her knowledge of the other islands in the Hawaiian chain was limited to their names. And she was pretty sure she didn't even know all of those.

"So, are you ready to tell me what I want to know?" he asked.

"I'd tell you if I knew anything. Please, you have to believe me."

"I don't have to believe you, actually. I just have to wait you out."

"What, what are you going to do to me?" she asked, hating herself for asking when she knew she wasn't going to want to hear the answer.

He smiled at her. "Nothing. I don't have to, after all. We are in no danger of discovery."

"But, you can't keep me here indefinitely," she said.

"Trust me, my dear, I don't plan to keep you here very long at all. As I'm sure you've realized by now, you're dehydrated. The human body can only go so long without water before organs begin to fail. After that comes death. So, I figure in a day or two you'll be willing to tell me anything I want to know."

"I'd tell you now. Please. I have no idea why you think that I was a courier."

He just shook his head. "I'm sure you'll see things my way, in time."

He turned and left the room. She shouted after him. "I don't know anything!"

It was no use.

Once again she went back to testing the strength of her bonds. There was still no give, nothing. She wanted to cry, but she remembered his words about dehydration. She didn't dare.

She had been thirsty before but now knowing his plan it seemed to somehow make the thirst worse.

It's because I know I won't be able to drink anything soon, she realized.

A soda commercial came on television and she screamed in rage and frustration. He had left the light on and she probed the room once more with her eyes, looking for something, anything she could use to try and free herself.

There was nothing in the room except her, the chair, and the television mounted on the wall where it met the ceiling. She stared at the closed closet door and wondered if she could make it over there and if there was anything inside that would make the effort worthwhile.

The chair she was tied to wasn't large or heavy but it was metal. There was no breaking it. The thinnest of seat cushions was on it, not enough to make for real comfort.

The floor of the room was wood, some sort of bamboo she thought. Her feet were lashed too tightly to the chair and at an awkward angle so she couldn't use them to push against the floor and slide herself across.

"God, help me do this, help them find me," she prayed. She took a deep breath, tensed all her muscles and tried to jump upwards, getting the chair to hop about half an inch in the direction she wanted to go. It jarred every bone in her body and she winced in pain.

She did it three more times in rapid succession and then had to stop. She was panting with the exertion and she realized she was even more dehydrated than she had thought she was. She had gained a total of two inches in her journey across the floor.

Jeremiah went back to his room. It was before six in the morning. There wasn't much he could do for another couple of hours. He needed to go to Pearl Harbor and retrace her footsteps from there. The police would be questioning everyone at the hotel to find out if they had seen or heard anything around the time Cindy had been kidnapped. There was nothing he could do there without ending up with Kapono shadowing his every move. It was a better use of his time to start at the beginning and work forward as the police worked backward. He turned on a morning news program and laid down to get a quick nap in.

He was just drifting off to sleep when he heard the newscaster say "In local news, a tourist is missing. Police are asking for any help locating this woman."

Jeremiah opened his eyes. There on the television was a picture of Cindy. He sat up and stared intently at the television while the newscaster finished the story. When it was done he turned the television off and tried to resist punching the wall behind it.

Now the kidnappers would know that people were looking for them. By plastering Cindy's picture all over the news the police knew they could have thousands of pairs of eyes looking for her. Which was all the more reason for the kidnappers to bury her. Maybe literally.

He stood up. He had less time than he'd thought. He was going to have to go to Pearl Harbor now. He grimaced. He would have to stop off at a store and buy some different clothes if he expected to be breaking onto a military base.

11

Mark woke in the morning with worry for Cindy and Jeremiah still gnawing at him. There was little he could do for them, though. He got up and a few minutes later was at his computer again searching the database of The National Center for Missing and Exploited Children hoping to find someone who looked like the Paul that he had known. He had already done an exhaustive search of kids kidnapped in California that would be the right age and he was expanding it to the rest of the country. Of course this was all assuming that whoever the real Paul was he had been reported missing and a body had never been found.

It was exhausting, depressing work and did nothing to help his mood. He had found an old newspaper article about the real Paul who had been kidnapped and then returned to his family a couple of years later. It at least gave him an age range to play around with. He still had no way of knowing whether his Paul had known he was a changeling although it seemed likely that he did.

The database did a great job trying to age photos so you could see what the missing kids would look like as adults. Try as he could, though, he couldn't find anyone who looked like his partner. When he finally closed down the website in frustration he realized that he wasn't going to find Paul that way. Either police had thought they recovered the correct body and taken him off the missing list or he had never been reported missing in the first place. The latter seemed outrageous, but it was possible he could have been a son of one of the cult members who had been drawn to the area.

Mark opened up a browser window and started a new search on the cult that had lived up in the mountains around the Green Pastures area where the bodies had been found.

The cult had been named the Jewels of Heaven. Rumor had it that they had converted much of their wealth into gold and jewels which they kept buried. He didn't know if they took their name from the buried jewels or if the name of the cult itself incited the rumors about buried treasure. It seemed that every decade or so someone went looking for it in a serious way only to come up empty-handed.

The leader of the cult had been a man named Matthew, from all accounts your typical charismatic psychopath. He had been a suspect in the kidnappings of some children from wealthy families, but nothing could ever be pinned on him and despite hefty ransoms being paid the children were never seen from again. The real Paul was one of those. Mark couldn't help but wonder if the bodies of the other kids would turn up in that same pit.

After three years the cult seemed to vanish without a trace. None of its members were seen or heard from again, including Matthew. With the ransom money he had gotten from the kids' families he could have easily fled south of the border and been living the high life somewhere in South America.

It was fascinating reading, but none of it explained where Not Paul could have come from or who he might have been before. He wrote down the names of the other kids who had been kidnapped. Rose Ayers, Danny Monroe, Sandra Colbert, and Jesse Armstrong. A quick search online revealed nothing about them in the years since their kidnappings were newsworthy. The one exception was a memorial service held seven years later for Danny Monroe on what would have been his twelfth birthday. At the age of five, Danny had been the youngest of the kidnapped kids.

Mark stared at the list and then reluctantly picked up the phone and dialed Harry, the coroner who had been the one to tell him that his partner had not been the real Paul Dryer. When the man picked up Mark felt himself gripping the phone tighter. He was still on suspension and it wouldn't look good for him if he was caught investigating anything more than the channel line-up on his television.

"Hi, Harry, it's Mark."

"Mark! Good to hear from you. Have they let you back in yet?"

"No, not yet. I'm working on it, though. Doing my therapy hours."

"I feel your pain."

"Yeah. Listen, Harry, I've got a favor to ask."

"Is it one that's going to get us both in trouble?"

"Probably," Mark admitted.

"Then let's hear it."

"I've been thinking a lot about what you told me about Paul, doing some digging of

185

my own. There were a bunch of other kids that the cult was rumored to have kidnapped back in the day. I was wondering if they are among the bodies you found in that mass grave."

There was a pause on the other end of the line and Mark began to worry that Harry wasn't going to help him. Finally the coroner broke the silence. "What are the names?"

"Rose Ayers, Danny Monroe, Sandra Colbert, and Jesse Armstrong."

"Okay, give me a minute."

Mark waited, listening to the sound of papers being shuffled. Finally Harry picked the phone back up. "I can confirm that the bodies of Rose Ayers and Jesse Armstrong were among those discovered."

"But not the others?"

"No. We finished identifying the last body a week ago and they were definitely not there."

Mark nodded. "Have Rose and Jesse's families been notified yet?"

"It was my understanding that they were. We haven't released any of the remains yet. We were planning to start doing that next week."

"Thanks, Harry. I owe you."

"Yeah you do. Never fear, though, I'm

sure I'll figure out a way for you to pay me back."

Mark hung up and crossed out Rose and Jesse's names on his list. That left Sandra and Danny, still missing. They were presumed dead, but why hadn't their bodies been recovered with the others? Had they been killed at a different time, dumped someplace else?

"Mark, under no circumstances should you go and talk to their families. It's a dumb idea which will reopen old wounds and bring them pain and land you in hot water," he told himself sternly.

A minute later he shook his head as he stood up from his desk. It looked like he was about to go and do something stupid.

Under cover of darkness Jeremiah had managed to slip onto the naval base. He was dressed in all black, flat and dull with nothing shiny, not even a button, visible. It would make it harder for human eyes to see him and impossible to tell crucial details like his height if he was caught on surveillance cameras. That was why so many with dark purposes chose the color of night, but few knew how to really utilize it to its fullest potential, understand the principles of physics that were in play and the way that light truly functioned. These things had long ago become second nature to him.

He moved swiftly from shadow to shadow, his rubber soled shoes silent as they touched the ground. Most personnel were asleep still and he took his time avoiding the sentries. He made his way to the public areas, circling the closed gift shop and standing for a moment staring at the shuttle that took tourists to the Arizona memorial.

He saw nothing out of the ordinary, certainly nothing that Cindy would see that dozens of others wouldn't. Satisfied that nothing in the immediate vicinity had something to do with her kidnapping he began walking, as he was told she had, off base toward Uncle's restaurant. He walked slowly. Kapono had said that it was highly unusual that the taxi driver would have directed her this way. He also knew that the driver was under suspicion and that the police were still trying to track him down.

He kept his head swiveling left and right, wondering what Cindy could have possibly seen that day. He was walking close to the water and he turned and glanced at it. Something made him stop and the hair on the back of his neck raised slightly. There was something not right about what he was seeing and he struggled to put his finger on it even as he strained his eyes.

He heard a soft splashing sound and he stepped closer. Something dark was bobbing on the surface of the water. He heard more splashing and he dropped to the ground, making himself that much more difficult to detect as he crawled closer. As he peered into the water he finally made out a low rubber raft bobbing on the surface of the water.

A man inside was dressed in black, but the gloves that he was wearing were shiny, reflecting the moonlight, and he wore a shark's tooth necklace, the white from the tooth standing out in stark contrast.

The man in the raft picked up a box and eased it over the side of the boat and dropped it in. That was the source of the splashing sounds. Jeremiah watched intently as the man dropped in several more packages. A minute after the last one was dumped a second man emerged from the water wearing a black wetsuit and scuba gear.

"Hurry up," he could hear the man on the boat whisper as he helped haul the other one up.

"It's done," the diver said after removing his breather and mask.

"You secured them good?"

"Same as always. No floating to the surface to cause problems, but easily removed when they come for them."

"I don't like it. Too many things going on lately. We need to tell them this will be the last shipment. At least until things settle."

"Are you an imbecile?" the diver asked, heat flooding his voice as he raised it slightly. "You know who we're dealing with. There's no getting out temporarily with them. There's just partnership and getting fed to the sharks off the coast of Ni'ihau."

"They wouldn't dare."

"If you think that you're more of an idiot than I thought you were. Let's get out of here."

Jeremiah tensed. He could hear their voices clearly, but could not see their faces. There was no way to get a better look, though, without exposing himself. He grit his teeth, wishing he could risk it. Instead he waited and watched as the boat moved away. Once they were gone he turned his attention back to the water where they had been dumping the boxes.

He weighed his options, briefly considering calling in Kapono. But getting the proper clearances and paperwork to go into the water on a naval base would take far too long. Whatever they were doing it was possible that Cindy might have seen or heard something, or that someone thought she did.

He pulled a small light out of his pocket that he had picked up in case he needed it. It was water proof as well, the shop that he had been able to purchase his things from carried mostly dive and surf equipment. He took off his shoes, put his cellphone beside them and after a moment's hesitation the dive knife he had got at the surf shop as well, and eased himself into the water as quietly as he could.

It was warmer than he anticipated and he was grateful. He swam out the few yards to where the diver had been. Then he took a deep breath and dove down, kicking hard. Once he was underwater he clicked on the light which illuminated the water below him. He kicked harder, heading downward. He finally saw a large pile of packages underneath a net that was weighted down. He managed to lift up a corner and pull one of the packages free. That done he headed for the surface as quickly as he could.

He hoisted himself up out of the water and put his shoes back on. He studied the package for a moment. It was about the size of a shoe box wrapped in plain brown paper.

He hooked a fingernail under a corner of the wrapping and tore it open.

When he finally opened the lid he saw that the box was filled with bags of a white looking powder. He stared at it for a moment. Drugs. They were dumping drugs into the harbor.

He picked up his cell and called Kapono.

"Hello?" the Detective asked after the fourth ring, sounding like he had been woken from sleep.

"It's Jeremiah. I think I found something interesting down at the naval base."

"Pearl Harbor?" Kapono asked. "What are you doing there at this hour? Base is closed to visitors."

"Never mind that," Jeremiah said. "But you need to get down here. Someone is using it as a dumping ground for drugs. I'm guessing it's part of a smuggling ring. I'm also guessing that Cindy saw something she shouldn't have when she was here."

"Then why wait so long to snatch her?" Kapono asked. "They took her nearly thirty-six hours later."

"Maybe it took that long to find her or maybe she did or said something else that caught their attention. Regardless, you want to know about the drugs or not?"

"Yes. Sorry, where are you?"

Jeremiah described his location.

"And how did you get there?"

"You don't want to know. And, Detective?"

"Yes."

"Keep my name out of it."

"I'm not sure I can —"

Jeremiah ended the call. He tossed the package back into the water. He pulled on his shoes, pocketed the dive knife and his phone and continued on the path he had been heading before he saw the men with the boat.

Within a few moments he made it to the restaurant. He stood outside for a moment before walking all around the building, taking everything in. The sun was rising. Police tape covered the front door. He ducked underneath it and entered.

The light was beginning to stream through the windows. Cindy had been here, stumbling into yet another crime scene. He closed his eyes and imagined her face, her scream, as she found the body.

And this time I wasn't here to come to her aid. I should have never let her go. He balled his hand into a fist and leaned his forehead against it even as he forced himself to breathe. He had known her for just over a year now and the way he felt about her was something new for him. New and dangerous for both of them.

It's time I leave, he realized. *Once I get her safely back home I need to leave town, head for a different state.*

It was going to be hard to start over in a new town with a new synagogue, but he had become far too entangled where he was. There were too many people he cared about, and too many who cared about him. Then there was the man from his past who had ended up dead on his lawn. When he thought about it, leaving was the only rational decision to be made.

But first, he would see Cindy safely home. He opened his eyes and began to look around. The place looked like a dive, hardly the sort of establishment a taxi driver would likely send a tourist, good food or no.

Kapono had said that they suspected that the owner was involved in illegal activity, specifically laundering drug money. Was he connected to whoever was dumping the drugs in the harbor? It seemed likely. And the taxi driver was likely involved as well. He knew that Kapono had said they hadn't yet run down the driver.

He walked around slowly, eyes sweeping everything as he tried to put himself in Cindy's shoes, see what she had seen. According to Kapono the restaurant had been empty when Cindy entered. He finally made his way to the kitchen. The chalk outline of a man and blood stains were on the floor. Jeremiah walked around the kitchen looking at it from every angle.

If Uncle had been killed by one of his partners or a rival it was likely for some reason. Maybe he had been cheating his partners or a rival wanted to take over his business. He knew that the police had already checked the man's home thoroughly for any evidence linking him to money laundering or drug trafficking. According to Kapono they had come up empty.

Which lead Jeremiah to believe that if the man had been keeping any kind of records they were right there in the restaurant. A box of disposable gloves was sitting on the counter. At least it looked like Uncle had taken what little food preparation he did seriously.

Jeremiah slid on a pair of gloves and then began to systematically check the kitchen. He did a cursory check of all the cabinets for false bottoms or backs. He checked underneath all the counters and behind the sink. He was moving toward the refrigerator when he heard the front door open.

He froze, listening. He heard footsteps in

the dining room, a single person, long stride, a big guy walking with confidence not sneaking around.

Jeremiah called out, "I'm in the kitchen, Kapono."

A moment later Kapono popped his head in the kitchen.

"What are you doing in here?" the detective asked.

"You found me here, what do you imagine I'm doing?" Jeremiah asked.

"Looking for more clues about Cindy's kidnapping."

Jeremiah nodded.

"How did you know it was me?"

Jeremiah shrugged. "Lucky guess."

"Yeah, right. You know you shouldn't be here. This is breaking and entering."

"Actually just entering. The door was open."

"Fine. We've got divers bringing up those packages you found in the harbor."

"I watched a couple of men dumping them. Didn't get a good look at them, but I'd recognize their voices if I heard them again."

"What I don't understand is why they were dumping the drugs."

"Well, since they were keeping them pinned down they weren't disposing of them, more like saving them for pick-up at a later time."

"Why bother?"

"Maybe that's how they handle the exchange," Jeremiah suggested.

"Complicated way to do things."

"Depends on the parties involved," Jeremiah said.

Kapono nodded. "So, what are we looking for?"

"We'll know when we find it," Jeremiah said. He moved to the refrigerator, opened it and looked through it. Then he opened the freezer.

"What you looking for in there? Trust me, you don't want to eat anything Uncle cooked."

"Maybe not, but I think I found something," Jeremiah said. He was staring in the freezer. There underneath a pig's head was something long and flat. He pulled it out. It was a clear pouch. He opened the pouch and pulled out a sheaf of papers.

He flipped through them quickly and then handed them to Kapono.

The detective whistled. "Lots of transactions here."

"Yeah, but I don't see any names."

"No, but there's some Hawaiian here, no names, but descriptions."

"What do they say?" Jeremiah asked.

"Ugly shows up a number of time. Bad leg too."

"Designations, nicknames perhaps?" Jeremiah asked.

"Could be. Here's one that shows up over and over again. Big boat man."

"Boat. What kind of boat I wonder?"

"Big. So, not an outrigger or a catamaran. Maybe more like a yacht," Kapono ventured.

"Got any yacht owners you suspect are involved with the drug trade?"

"A couple."

"Here's another one. Kama'aina. It shows up a few times, but it looks like more money was going to whoever that it is than was coming from them."

"Something Uncle was funding perhaps?"

"I don't know."

"What does Kama'aina mean?" Jeremiah asked.

"Of the land. It's a term for locals."

Kapono flipped through the rest of the pages quickly and then looked up with a frustrated sigh.

"What's wrong?"

"I was hoping for account numbers. But I don't see any here."

"Maybe they're encoded too."

"Yeah, maybe. Or maybe he got those from someone else."

Jeremiah cocked his head.

Kapono scowled. "The card the taxi driver gave Cindy to give to Uncle wasn't a normal business card. It had a string of numbers on it. Maybe he was the one supplying account numbers for Uncle to move the money into or out of."

"Whoever kidnapped Cindy might think she has the account numbers," Jeremiah said.

Kapono shook his head. "Then let's hope they don't figure out she doesn't. If they do they have no reason to keep her alive."

Jeremiah set his jaw. "But if they think she has them, they'll be torturing her for them."

"I don't want to think about that," Kapono said.

"We need to find that taxi driver."

"He won't know where she is."

"No, but he'll know who else is involved who might know what happened to her."

"You're right. We should get out of here. I have to check in with my captain. This whole thing just got a whole lot bigger than a missing persons case now that we can definitely tie her kidnapping in with the murder."

"First we need to make sure we didn't

miss anything else," Jeremiah said.

"Okay, where do we look next?"

Fifteen minutes later Jeremiah was satisfied that there was nothing left in the restaurant to find. Kapono had the good sense not to ask how Jeremiah knew to check some of the obscure locations he did.

"I think we're done here," Jeremiah told Kapono. The detective nodded and together they headed to the front of the restaurant. The sun was shining brightly through the windows making the place look that much worse. As they neared the door Jeremiah slowed, letting Kapono go first.

The big detective swung the door open wide and ducked underneath the police tape. Before he could straighten up a shot rang out. Jeremiah dropped to the ground and watched as Kapono teetered for a moment before crumbling to the ground in front of him.

12

Cindy had managed to make it to the closet by jolting her chair an inch at a time closer. She was sweating and shaking from the exertion and the thirst had become unbearable. The closet had a sliding door. She leaned her head against it and pushed toward the side. It opened a crack, just enough for her to wiggle a finger into it and push. It slid open a little more and she kept working at it until she could see the entire inside of the closet.

It was empty.

She leaned her head against the wall, sobbing in frustration.

Keep going, a voice inside her head seemed to say.

She turned her head toward the door. She had to make it out of the room. Somewhere in the house there had to be something she could use to help free herself.

She coiled all her muscles and lurched

sideways in the chair.

Jeremiah could hear Kapono groaning which meant the detective was still alive. He had no idea how badly he was hit, though. Jeremiah slid to the side, out of direct line of sight of the door. Kapono moved, reaching for the gun that was in his waistband.

Jeremiah pulled the dive knife out of his pocket with his right hand and slid it out of its sheath. He waited, listening, and watching.

Outside the door Jeremiah heard boots crunching on the ground.

"We can't kill him," someone hissed.

"We have to. He's seen us," a second voice answered and Jeremiah recognized it as the diver from the harbor.

"We have to get out of here. The cops found the drop spot. It's all over." The speaker was definitely the other man from the harbor, the one who had remained in the boat.

"Nothing's over. There's nothing to tie it to us. We just have to keep cool and take care of business."

Jeremiah could see the legs of one of them at last. He was fairly certain it was the diver, the one who was insisting that they finish

Kapono off. Kapono's hand was behind his back, wrapped around the butt of his gun and Jeremiah wasn't sure if the assailant could see it from where he was.

The man squatted down and took the sheaf of papers from Kapono's hand. Jeremiah had a clear shot at the man's chest, but hesitated. If he killed him that would mean a world of headache, paperwork, and questions at the very least. All these things would slow down his search for Cindy, and the more questions people asked the more he risked being discovered for who he had been in his past.

No, he couldn't risk killing the man. But he could certainly wound him. He threw the knife and it embedded itself in the man's leg. He screamed and as he fell backwards Kapono freed his gun and fired. Jeremiah could see the body jerk as it fell.

"Don't move," Kapono warned, training his gun, presumably on the other man.

Jeremiah stood and crossed over to the doorway. The diver was dead, shot through the head. The second man stood a few feet back, hands in the air, a look of terror on his face. The clothes of both marked them as being members of the U.S. navy. Kapono had just shot a military man. There was going to be hell to pay over that one and

Jeremiah was exceedingly glad that it had been Kapono who killed the man and not Jeremiah.

"How badly are you hit?" he asked Kapono softly.

"Not badly enough that I'll miss killing this scum if he moves," Kapono said, voice grim.

Jeremiah leaned down and offered Kapono his hand, careful not to take his eyes off of the other man.

"I'll get myself up. Go check him for weapons," Kapono said.

Jeremiah moved forward and swiftly patted down the man. The last name embroidered on his uniform was Erickson. He had a handgun and a Swiss army knife on him which Jeremiah tossed back toward Kapono.

He glanced back and saw the detective getting to his feet. There was blood soaking his left shoulder. He tossed Jeremiah his handcuffs and Jeremiah cuffed the man, making sure he did it tight.

"That's too tight," Erickson protested. "You're cutting off my circulation."

Jeremiah didn't say a word. He had cuffed the man tight enough that it was highly unlikely he would be able to escape even if he did break his thumbs in an attempt to get free. He pushed Erickson down to a kneeling position, making sure he got a good eyeful of his dead buddy.

He glanced over at Kapono. He was pale and swaying slightly on his feet.

"Better call it in, and then sit down before you fall down," Jeremiah advised.

"Good idea," Kapono grunted. He took out his phone, called for an ambulance and back-up.

Jeremiah walked quickly over. He ripped the right sleeve off Kapono's shirt, wadded it into a ball and pressed it against the wound to help stop the bleeding.

"He just winged me," the detective grunted.

"Yeah, but I think it's more than a scratch."

Kapono took over the job of putting pressure on the wound.

"You're going to be okay until the ambulance gets here?"

"Yeah, why you ask?" Kapono asked, his accent slightly thicker.

Jeremiah didn't say anything. He turned and moved back to Erickson. The man looked up at him, apprehension in his eyes. Of the two men he had been the more cautious. Jeremiah leaned down so he was eye-to-eye with him.

"Tell me where Cindy is," he growled.

"Who?"

"I don't have time for this," Jeremiah, said backhanding the man.

The blow wasn't strong, just enough to really rattle him.

"Hey, you can't do that!" Erickson sputtered.

"And who's going to stop me? Who *could* stop me?" Jeremiah demanded, lowering his voice.

"I don't know any Cindy."

"Sure you do. She's the woman who found Uncle's body here the other day. She also spotted you and your buddy dumping drugs into the harbor on Saturday."

"Sat-Saturday. We weren't in port on Saturday. I wasn't here."

Jeremiah could read truth in the man's eyes.

"Tell me about this drug ring you've got going," Jeremiah said.

Blood was trickling at the side of Erickson's mouth where Jeremiah had struck him.

"Look, I know my rights —"

"You gave up all your rights when you became involved in all of this, when you came here and when you shot my friend over there. Now, the police will be here in a few minutes and I'm sure they'd be willing to cut you a deal. Accessory to attempted murder of an officer won't make you a popular man. I'm not interested in any of that, though, and mark my words, if you don't tell me what I want to know, I will kill you before they get here."

Erickson licked his lips and nodded slowly. "Look, I don't know much. We pick up the drugs, smuggle them back here, and then dump them in the harbor when we're in port. Someone else picks them up. That's all I know."

"Who is working with you?"

He gestured with his head to the dead man. "Daniels there. He brought me in. I never met anyone else. And he never said any names. He gave me my cut of the money after the job was done."

Just their luck Kapono had killed the man with the information. Jeremiah ground his teeth in frustration. "You don't have any clue who the guys who bring the drugs up are?"

Erickson shook his head. "They're not military, that's all I know."

"Any chance they were bringing up a shipment last Saturday?"

"It's possible. We'd dumped some there about a week ago. It was only a short cruise out this time on maneuvers."

"So, where did you get the shipment of drugs you were dumping this morning?"

"It was the other half of the shipment from last week. We could only make one run before we went out for the maneuvers."

Jeremiah believed him. It seemed that whoever had decided Cindy was a risk hadn't been either of these guys. By the sounds of things, there hadn't been anyone in Uncle's when she found the body. So, unless a cop was involved, he needed to keep searching for whoever it was who had targeted her.

He could hear sirens approaching. He glanced over at Kapono. He was still conscious. He nodded at Jeremiah, seeming to understand what he was about to do. Jeremiah turned and jogged away, mind racing. He had gone about a mile when he stripped off the plastic gloves he was still wearing and dumped them in a trash bin behind another restaurant.

He had left no fingerprints on the knife embedded in the dead man's leg. Even if he had, they would never find a match to them in any of their computers. He went back through Cindy's schedule in his mind. It was still possible that she had seen the guys who were retrieving the drugs when she had visited Pearl Harbor.

From the receipts he'd found in her room he knew she'd had some sushi at the International Marketplace and then gone to a luau on the north shore. In his mind the boat excursion with the near drowning and the faulty life preserver seemed a much more likely place to find information about her kidnapper, particularly since it was much closer in time to the kidnapping than either of the other events.

What would be really helpful is if they could find the taxi driver who had given Cindy the card to give to Uncle. But Kapono had told him the night before that they hadn't been able to turn up any leads on the man. Wiki Taxi had no records of any of their drivers doing a pickup at Cindy's hotel at the time in question. So, he had told Jeremiah there was an officer combing through the list of drivers trying to see who had verified pickups at about that time who could be ruled out as possible suspects. That kind of work could be invaluable, but the clock was ticking and they were running out of time.

Jeremiah made a snap decision to break with following the pattern and skip to the boat trip. He could double back and check out the Marketplace and the luau later if he turned up empty there.

Another mile and he was able to flag down a taxi who was happy to take him to the harbor used by the snorkeling tour. The sun was up and shining brightly, but the boat hadn't yet left for the morning. He found the man in charge of checking passengers onto the boat.

"Name?" the man in the blue polo shirt asked, pen poised above his clipboard.

"Not important. I'm here to ask questions about one of your passengers from a couple of days ago, Cindy Preston."

"Cindy Preston. Oh, yeah, I heard on television this morning she'd been kidnapped," the guy said, eyes widening.

"That's right," Jeremiah said.

"Sorry to hear that. Yeah, I recognized her name. She was on one of our cruises on Sunday. Turning out to be a very unlucky cruise that one."

"Why?" Jeremiah asked.

"A lady almost drowned on that cruise. The life preserver she was using was faulty. Instead of holding her up it started dragging her under. Another passenger heard her screaming, our guys jumped into the water. They had to cut the life preserver off her."

"It wasn't Cindy?"

"No. Another lady. They took her to the

hospital afterward. From what I heard the whole thing was just bizarre. I've never heard of a life preserver malfunctioning like that. It's the darndest thing."

It sounded to Jeremiah like someone had been trying to use that life preserver to kill someone. The question was, who was the intended target? Was it the woman who had nearly drowned or was it Cindy? And if the other woman was the target, did Cindy witness something she shouldn't have?

"Can you tell me the name of the woman who almost drowned?"

"Sure, just give me a couple of minutes."

"Any of your staff call in sick since then?" Jeremiah asked.

"No one's called in sick, but Al hasn't shown up. He was supposed to work the last two days."

"Do you have contact information for Al?"

"Yeah, sure. Are you with the police or something?" the man asked, finally realizing that something was wrong.

"Private investigator," Jeremiah lied.

The man turned pale. He was probably wondering if the company was about to be sued for what had happened to the woman who nearly drowned.

"I want to ask him some questions about Cindy. I think he might have been one of the last people to see her before she was kidnapped," Jeremiah said.

"Oh, well, of course. Give me just a minute."

The man scurried away and Jeremiah stood, eyes roving around the dock, taking everything in. A couple of minutes later the man returned with two pieces of paper. "That's Al's address. The other is the name and hotel for the lady who almost drowned. Just in case you need it. Marge Johnson at the Royal Hawaiian."

"Thanks," Jeremiah said, taking the papers.

He grabbed another taxi and had it drop him a couple of blocks away from Al's house. He didn't want the man to see him coming if he was home. The houses were a hodge-podge of styles and sizes. A rundown shack with dead cars out front was next door to a three-story mansion. Jeremiah had never seen anything quite like it.

The house he was looking for turned out to be modest, but kept up well. There was no car parked out front, but there was a garage, something half the houses on the street didn't seem to have. Jeremiah could see a car inside.

Jeremiah walked cautiously around the house, looking and listening for anything out of the ordinary. He could hear no television or talking inside the house. Several windows were open, screens intact. It was completely silent from within.

Jeremiah found a sliding glass door in the back. He cautiously peered through it, but could see no one. He finally tried the door and it slid easily. He slipped inside, closing it silently behind himself. He was standing in a living room. There was a surfing board acting as a coffee table with a scattering of surf magazines on top of it. A large, flat screen television graced one wall and an impressive array of stereo equipment was piled on tables beside it.

Jeremiah crept down the hall to the right and found himself in a bedroom. Clothes were piled in a corner, including a similar blue polo shirt to the one he'd seen the cruise company representative wearing. In the closet he found a black wetsuit and other dive gear. On an island that was not such an unusual discovery, especially given that the guy worked on a snorkeling tour boat. He might at one point have led dives as well.

Jeremiah moved quickly through the rest of the rooms, but there was no one in the house. He then started systematically check- ing for anything the guy might have hidden like money or drugs. In a foot locker underneath the bed he found a variety of weapons including knives and guns including a spear gun. Again it wasn't damning evidence, especially for life in the islands. He had once worked with a Hawaiian and he knew that all kids who grew up in the islands were taught how to shoot in high school. Hunting was still a big part of the culture, too.

Jeremiah kept going, searching room by room for anything illegal. By the time he made it to the kitchen he was running out of hope. If Al was involved he wasn't keeping any of the contraband in his house. He began to wonder if maybe he had the wrong guy.

It was possible that whatever had happened on that cruise had been an accident, or that someone else had intended to hurt Marge or Cindy or even someone else entirely with the life preserver. He was regretting that he hadn't demanded a list of addresses for all the crew and passengers from that day. If he headed back to the docks he'd have a chance to question any of the crew that had been on the ship that day when the current day's cruise returned.

You're moving too fast, getting sloppy, he muttered to himself.

He had nearly finished searching the

kitchen when he stopped to take a deep breath. There was nowhere else inside the house to search. He could try the grounds next, but doubted he'd find anything. The last cupboard he checked had baking supplies, flour, sugar, and the like. He stared at them for a moment. He hadn't seen a single cake pan or muffin tin anywhere else in the kitchen. It was possible Al was using the ingredients for things like pancakes, but there were very few specialty items in his kitchen. Why would he go to the trouble of making something like that from scratch? Why not just buy a mix and add water?

He pulled the sugar bag out of the cabinet and opened it. He tasted the contents. Definitely sugar. He was about to put it back when on a hunch he plunged his hand down into the bag. His fingers brushed something that felt like plastic. He pulled it out. The object was a small sandwich bag filled with white powder. Drugs. He'd bet his life on it.

He put them back and then grabbed the flour bag. Inside it he could feel another plastic bag. This one contained a wad of hundred dollar bills the size of his fist. Emergency money in case he had to escape quickly.

And it was still here. Meaning, Al hadn't

fled. There were no signs of a struggle so odds were he hadn't been taken either. So, where was he?

It confirmed his suspicions that Al was involved with the drug smugglers. It was possible he was one of the ones who picked up the drugs once they were dumped in the harbor. It was possible he knew Cindy had seen him there. And when she recognized him on the tour boat he tried to kill her and somehow Marge got in the way.

He knew he was jumping to conclusions, but they fit with what he knew. The more time he wasted the less chance he had of saving Cindy.

Jeremiah closed the cupboard and turned toward the kitchen table. A gun case was on the table, opened. Jeremiah examined it. It was meant to house a smaller handgun, easily concealable on someone's person. There was an open box of bullets beside it. Given that the gun was missing and that these things weren't with the other weapons in the foot locker, Jeremiah guessed that wherever Al was he had the loaded gun on him.

What are you doing with the gun, Al? Jeremiah wondered. His stomach tightened into knots as he thought of Cindy. Was Al going to finish the job and kill her? His car was in the garage. Did he have another one or had he walked to wherever he was going?

A thousand questions raced through Jeremiah's mind as he struggled to regain his composure. He thought of the guns in the other room and it was all he could do to keep himself from going and getting one of them. He couldn't be caught with it, though, no matter what.

His eyes fell on the other items on the kitchen table. There was a half drunk glass of milk. He stared at it a moment and then realized there was condensation on the outside of the glass. Wherever Al had gone, he must have left shortly before Jeremiah got there. Which meant there might be time to catch him if only he knew where he was going.

A notepad was sitting out next to the glass, a pen beside it. Jeremiah picked it up. The top piece of paper bore the imprints from what had been written on the one above it.

Marge Johnson. Royal Hawaiian Hotel room 634. The woman who almost drowned.

Jeremiah closed his fist around it. He now knew where Al was. He had gone to kill Marge Johnson.

13

Cindy's vision was swimming. She desperately wished she could rest, but with the television blaring there was no real sleep to be had. The thirst and exhaustion and the sheer pain of jolting the metal chair across the floor made her sob, but no tears came, further proof of her dehydration. But, she couldn't rest, she had to press on because she had no idea how long before one of her captors would return. Plus, she had a horrible, creeping feeling that if she did manage to fall asleep she would never wake up again.

Every second felt like it might be her last as she wondered if she'd even be able to hear a door close or any other sign that someone was coming back to question her further. She could see the logic in their methods. Given how badly she was shaking and how much the deprivations were crushing her she would have gladly told them anything. Unfortunately the one thing they wanted to know seemed to be the one thing she knew nothing about. The irony was not lost on her.

She finally made it to the door. She didn't know how long the journey from the closet had taken. Minutes? Hours? She studied the door for a moment, looking for anything that might help her, a rough bit of wood or a nail perhaps. She nudged it slightly so she could crane her neck and get a look at the inside of the door.

There was a mirror. She blinked at it for a moment, mind fuzzy, trying to comprehend why she felt a sudden surge of excitement. And then it came to her. If she could smash it, she could use the shards of glass to saw through her ropes. She stared at it intently, willing herself to think and cursing the fog that seemed to be descending on her.

Smash it, ram it with something, anything, your head, she urged herself.

But another voice whispered caution. If she did this wrong she risked cutting herself badly and possibly bleeding to death. For one crazed minute she thought that at least that would be quicker than the dehydration death Mr. Black had described.

No, she couldn't ram it with her own body, and even if she wanted to risk it she might not be able to slam it hard enough to break it. The chair, on the other hand, was metal, plenty hard. She shoved the door with her fingers, trying to get it closed so that it wouldn't be able to move.

Once she had accomplished that she contorted in the chair, turning it around an inch at a time and closer to the mirror. When at last her back was to the mirror, and she was just a couple of inches away from it she shifted her weight forward and then threw it backwards, trying to cause the chair to tilt.

It moved slightly, but not enough. She rocked forward, heart stuttering as she felt the back legs come off the ground. Then she threw herself backwards again and the back legs crashed down even as the front ones came up. It still wasn't enough.

"Please, God," she prayed silently as she rocked forward again, nearly losing her balance and falling forward but catching herself just in time to send herself backward and as the chair tilted back she remembered just in time to lean her head forward so it, too, wouldn't slam into the mirror.

The back of the chair struck the mirror with a cracking sound. It wasn't enough to merely crack the mirror, though. As soon as the front legs came back down she continued her rocking and smashed into the mirror again. The cracking was much more ominous and she bit her lip, tasting blood. Once more she rocked forward and then back.

The chair struck the mirror and suddenly the sound of shattering glass was overpowering as it all came down, raining onto her and the floor, shattering into smaller and ever small pieces. She felt tiny shards embed themselves in her legs and she cried out with the pain, her voice hoarse and unrecognizable even to her own ears.

She looked down, there were a couple of large pieces on her lap, but she couldn't reach them with either hand. There was no way she could manipulate her legs with the way they were bound to the chair in order to help. She looked down at the floor and all the other shards that were out of reach.

If they couldn't come to her, she would have to go to them. Before she could change her mind she threw herself sideways in the chair. She did it with enough force that she went over, crashing to the ground. She landed hard on her right shoulder and heard a sickening popping sound. Pain knifed through her and she squinted against it. She had bit the inside of her cheek as well and the blood welled up in her mouth.

By a miracle she had landed with her fingers within reach of a particularly long and jagged shard of mirror. She grasped it between her thumb and forefinger and was able to twist it around to bring it against the ropes around her wrist. She began to saw back and forth flexing her wrist as much as she could and manipulating the shard with the two fingers.

Back and forth she sawed as time seemed to stand still. She could smell the blood in her mouth and the glass embedded in her legs burned like fire, but none of it was anything compared to the pain that flooded her shoulder. It was throbbing now and it was becoming harder and harder to control and manipulate the shard of mirror.

Her arm was probably broken, she realized, struggling not to let the pain overcome her completely. The first strand of the rope began to fray beneath the constant sawing motion. If only she could make bigger sweeps or apply more pressure it would go faster, but she would do what she could, praying it would be enough in the end.

A sudden slamming sound somewhere else in the house caused her to freeze for a moment in terror. She stared toward the door, expecting it to fly open at any minute and Mr. Black or one of his associates to come in and catch her.

Move faster, a voice seemed to whisper inside her head. It made sense. If someone was in the house she needed to do everything she could to free herself before they came back to check on her.

She sawed away frantically and she began to feel the rope give. She strained, trying to break it, even as she kept sawing away. Finally the strand she was working on gave way with a snap. She wiggled her wrist, pulling at the rope, and she felt it slacking.

She twisted her wrist back and forth until it was coated in blood. The lubricant helped her and she finally managed to pull her wrist free of the restraints. With a gasp she picked the shard back up and moved it over to her other hand. It felt so amazing to be able to move even that much, but the stabbing pain in her arm reminded her of her injury.

She sawed away at a strand of the robe binding her left hand and because she had more motion and pressure she could bring to it the rope began to give away much faster. The rope finally snapped and she was able to yank that hand free as well. She twisted on the floor so that she could reach the ropes binding her legs. She felt the knot and realized after a moment that she wouldn't be able to untie it.

The shard again went to work, this time in her left hand as she kept her right arm as still as she could. Because her feet were completely numb she had to saw through three strands before she was able to move them. Agony shot through her as she pulled them free and blood began to rush into them. She shook them hard, hoping that when she stood they would take her weight.

She wished she could take the time to pluck the slivers from her legs, but every second lost was a second closer to being discovered. She managed to turn over onto her stomach and she got her arms and legs under her and heaved up.

She collapsed almost instantly and she pounded the floor with her fist in rage and frustration. She reached out and grabbed the corner of the wall where it formed the closet and used it to help haul herself to her feet. She stamped her feet a couple of times as they came tingling back to life, praying that she would be able to walk.

Finally she let go of the wall. She tottered for a moment on legs that felt like jelly. She wasn't sure what was a result of the prolonged immobilization and what was a result of the lack of food, water and sleep. She took a step forward, knee nearly giving way beneath her. She grabbed the doorknob, though, and steadied herself. Then she eased the door open, holding her breath as she peered down the hallway.

A sudden high-pitched sound split the air around her, drowning out the television easily. It seemed to be coming from just outside the window in the room. She froze. Had she set off some kind of alarm system?

It blared loud and sharp, making her ears ache. And then, finally, it ended. She blinked, not sure what it was or what had caused it. Was it possible it was some sort of air raid siren, a natural disaster alert? She'd heard they used such a system in the islands.

If there was some sort of disaster, though, she didn't have time to worry about what it could be.

The hallway was empty. She could see a door on the left, a door at the far end which seemed to lead to another bedroom, a door on the right which she suspected was also a bedroom, and past that a hallway also heading off to the right.

She opened the door wide and stepped out into the hall, her hands on the walls to help balance herself. She debated closing the door. If Mr. Black saw it he would instantly know something was wrong, but if one of his associates was guarding her, he might not realize it was supposed to be open and it might buy her some more time.

After a moment's hesitation she shut the door most of the way so that noise from the television was still coming through clearly but anyone glancing casually that way wouldn't see the chair or the broken glass.

She walked down the hallway, pausing to peek around the corner of the bedroom on the right and a bathroom on the left. They were both empty. The bathroom didn't even have toilet paper in it. At the hallway she turned and kept going. A few feet and then the hallway let out into a great room meant to be kitchen, dining room and living room combined. Sliding glass doors were on the left, another hallway straight ahead. And to the right, next to the kitchen, was a front door with beveled glass.

She made her way toward it, her legs a little stronger. On the kitchen counter she saw several bottles of water. With a shaking hand she grabbed one and slid it into the pocket of her skirt. She wanted the others, wanted to stand there and drink her fill, but she had to keep going while she could. She thought about the thudding sound she had heard earlier. Maybe it had been someone leaving the house instead of entering.

Or maybe they were just in one of the other rooms she hadn't explored yet.

She reached the front door and twisted it open. It wasn't even locked. Mr. Black really wasn't worried about being disturbed there.

She opened it and stepped cautiously out onto a lanai. To the left was a door back into the other part of the house. To the right were the stairs that headed down to the ground and the open air carport underneath the house.

She lurched toward the stairs, grasping the banisters firmly in each hand. The pain in her right arm was becoming overwhelming and as she made it down the first two steps she was terrified that she was going to pass out.

There was a landing a little ways down and then the stairs twisted downward again. *You can make it, get to the landing,* she ordered herself. Each downward step felt like it jolted every bone in her body, like it was rattling them together. She could hear her breath coming as uneven gasps. The water bottle in her pocket banged against her leg, tempting her even while it weighed her down.

She made it to the landing, and turned slowly, and faced the last set of stairs. The carport was empty and so was what little she could see of the gravel driveway from where she was.

Hurry, Cindy, hurry and you're free, she told herself.

She pushed through the pain, taking each step as it came, until it seemed like all her life she had been climbing stairs and nothing else. When at last she reached the bottom she stood for a moment, afraid that if she let go of the railings she would fall.

But sooner or later she had to risk it. Sooner could save her life. She let go, tottering for a moment. She took a step forward, and then another, aiming for a line of trees just a few steps away. She made it and pushed through them. They were thick and close together, but she could still make her way through without too much effort.

A flash of yellow among the green caught her eye and she turned her head to see that she was nearly eye-level with a whole bunch of apple bananas. They were small, nearly ripe, and right there in front of her. A cluster of banana trees. That's what she was standing in.

She reached out and grabbed a banana and yanked it free. It was harder than she had anticipated and the effort almost knocked her over. But the fruit came free and she stuffed it and then a second one into her other pocket. Sticky sap coated her hands and she wiped it on her dress. She had already ruined Geanie's clothes anyway.

She pushed on farther, trying to get as much distance between herself and the house as she could. She wasn't thinking straight. She knew she should have headed toward the road where she could find another house, or a driver, and try to get help.

Of course, she might have run straight into Mr. Black that way. After it felt like she'd been walking for quite a while she stopped. She stood for a moment before her legs gave way and she landed on the ground, shaking and in pain. Her vision seemed to her to be fading, colors were losing their intensity, and her peripheral vision was gone.

I'm going to pass out, she realized.

And that's when she finally remembered the bottle of water. She reached into her pocket and pulled it out. She wrapped her left hand around the cap and tried to twist it off. Her entire body was shaking with the effort and she realized she didn't have the strength to open it.

"God, please, help me," she thought as she closed her eyes. She wrapped the skirt around the cap, reached deep inside herself and twisted with everything she had. It gave way and a moment later she was putting the bottle up to her lips.

Her tongue seemed to absorb the first drops that hit them, not even letting them pass to the back of her throat. She could feel her lips, dry, splitting. The water was warm but she had never tasted anything so wonderful, so refreshing. She drained the bottle and nearly became hysterical when she realized there wasn't any more.

She pulled the bananas out of her pocket and tried to peel the first one. It was just under ripe, though, and didn't want to peel easily. She dug her fingernail into the skin, trying to puncture it, but it wouldn't give. She brought the banana up to her mouth and bit down on the top as hard as she could. The taste of the peel nearly made her gag, but she spit it out and then ate the fruit. She did the same with the next one.

And slowly her vision seemed to come back to her. And with it her ability to think. There had to be a road somewhere nearby. She couldn't hear any passing traffic, but that could just mean that the area she was in was a little more isolated. She still had no clue which of the islands she was on, not that it would help her even if she did.

She stood slowly, and looked around. She didn't want to go back in the direction of the house, even if there was a road that way. If they had discovered she was gone they'd be searching for her and she refused to walk back into their arms.

The mountains she had been able to see from the house were behind her. It could be part of the volcano that had formed the island. If they were, they would form part of the center of the island. Which meant she should travel away from them, head for the ocean where the majority of the populace would be.

She pushed through the trees, looking for more bananas, but those trees seemed to have given way to palm trees. She forced herself to keep walking, wondering how far from the ocean she was.

A sound behind her caused her to pause, listening. Was it an animal, or was that a human footstep? Her heart began to pound in fear. Could they have found her already? She didn't hear it again and she kept walking, trying to step lightly, but she was too exhausted to do a good job of it. She picked up her pace, abandoning quiet for speed.

Again she heard a sound behind her, but this time she didn't stop, she began to move faster, grasping the trunks of the trees with her left hand as she pushed through them.

A sudden squealing sound to her left caused her to spin in that direction. A flash of brown caught her eye and a moment later she saw the tusk of a wild boar. She picked up her pace, even more eager to reach civilization.

The trees were becoming fewer. Surely that had to be a good sign. She pushed forward. There had to be a road soon, a house, something.

And then she saw a break in the tree line, and beyond it, nothing but blue as far as the eye could see. The ocean, it had to be. She limped toward it, aware that she was slowing down. What good the food and water had done couldn't compensate for her need to sleep and to heal.

Behind her she heard another step and then a crashing sound followed by a shout. With a gasp she lunged forward, pushing herself harder, praying that she could find the road before her hunters could find her.

She made it to the last tree and then looked around. All she saw in any direction was red dirt. No cars, no houses, no roads. She stared straight ahead and saw the ocean. She had made it, but why was no one around? She hurried toward it, knowing in the back of her mind that something was wrong, but she was too tired, too terrified to recognize what it was.

A minute later she figured it out. She was standing at the edge of a cliff. Below her was the ocean, no beach, just waves crashing against a few rocks. She stared in horror. She was trapped. The ocean was before her, a long drop beneath, and her enemies were behind. She twisted her head left and right looking to see where the cliff might start sloping down to the beach.

It was Hawaii after all, land of a thousand beaches. Where was one when she needed it? She could feel herself beginning to hyperventilate. The shouts were closer. They had found her, they were going to recapture her. There was nowhere she could run, they would be faster. There was nowhere she could hide. She was standing on a barren plateau with the nearest vegetation a hundred yards distant and not nearly thick enough to be lost within.

There was nowhere she could go but down. She stared at the face of the rock wall, searching for stairs, a pathway, anything. But the rock face was sheer, unforgiving. There was no way down.

Unless you jump.

Bile flooded her mouth and she backed away from the cliff, shaking.

No, never, I can't, she thought, her mind seeming to shatter. *It's too far, I could never survive it.*

Yes you could, the voice whispered again.

The rocks would crush her.

Not if you fall in the right place.

God, you can't ask me to do this. You know what happened last time. My sister . . . I can't.

"I can't!" she screamed, staggering away from the edge.

You must! Now!

"I can't, I'll fall," she whispered.

Let me catch you.

God was talking to her. She knew it, felt it. She had never heard His voice so clear. And He had never asked anything so impossible of her. She couldn't. Anything else, but not this, never this. She didn't want to jump, she couldn't.

And she heard her sister's voice in her mind, laughing, telling her that it was fine, that nothing was going to happen to her, that she should jump.

Her sister had never been more wrong.

But God had never been so insistent.

Jump! the voice commanded.

And the men were upon her, they would have her in a moment. She could hear at least two voices. One of them was Mr. Black. He was talking to her, but she was long beyond being able to hear him. There was nothing he could offer her, only more torture and death. She had nothing he wanted and he would figure that out sooner or later.

She couldn't go back to that room, that house, captivity and the endless, crushing pain and fear.

She stepped to the ledge, she looked down. Below the waves were crashing on the rocks.

She had to jump. There was no other way.

She closed her eyes and she jumped.

14

Cindy jumped, expecting to feel the rush of wind on her face and the sickening feeling in the pit of her stomach as she plunged off the cliff into the crushing waves of the ocean below. But instead she felt a hard hand clamp around her arm and yank her backward. She fell to the ground hard and opened her eyes to see the face of Mr. Black staring down at her. She could see fury burning in his eyes.

"You're either incredibly brave or incredibly stupid to try that," he said.

"Stupid," she heard herself whisper. It was absurd. He wasn't looking for an answer from her. What compelled her to give one anyway was beyond her.

"Clever, heading into the jungle instead of making for the highway. My sentry never even saw you."

She wanted to cry. If she had only listened to the voice, if only she had jumped sooner she might be free.

Or dead, she reminded herself.

"You have proven yourself to be quite resourceful . . . again. This now leaves me with the question of what to do with you."

And from the look on his face she was pretty sure that killing her on the spot was currently topping his list of options.

"Take me back to Oahu," she blurted out.

He raised an eyebrow. "And why on earth would I want to do that?"

"Because," she said, struggling for something to say, something that would buy her time and one more opportunity to escape or be rescued. "I can take you to where I hid it," she said. Her only value to him was in helping find whatever it was he was looking for.

"How about you just tell me where it is or I make things really unpleasant for you?"

She licked her cracked, bleeding lips. "More unpleasant than killing me?" she challenged, feeling like an idiot even as she heard the words coming out of her mouth. "I don't think so. And it would be too difficult to describe the location. And . . . and only I can retrieve it."

"I'm listening."

She felt panic flare in her. She was lying through her teeth, struggling to say things that sounded plausible. "I'm done talking until you get me back to Oahu." She pressed her lips together, hoping the symbolic gesture was not lost on him.

He pulled a knife out of his pocket and crouched down next to her. He placed the blade against her cheek and she forced herself to remain absolutely still and stare him in the eyes. She knew that if she flinched, even in the slightest, it was all over. He stared back at her, eyes hard and calculating. She wanted to blink, but she refused to let herself. It was like some of the insane staring contests she'd had with friends as a kid. She had always won. Now was not the time to start losing.

He blinked first. Slowly he stood up and pocketed his knife. "Okay, we'll play this your way. But if you so much as breathe wrong, I will kill you in the most unpleasant way I can think of. And trust me, you don't want to see just how creative I can get."

She nodded once, to show that she understood. There was a man she didn't recognize with Mr. Black and he came forward and hoisted her to her feet. He was a large, Hawaiian man, more muscle than fat. She studied his face, wondering what manner of man he was and if there was any way she could manipulate him into showing some pity. His expression was impossible to read, though.

"Can you please just not drug me again?" she asked Mr. Black.

Jeremiah arrived at the Royal Hawaiian, which the taxi driver was quick to inform him was a famous old hotel, a landmark. The hotel was pink. Jeremiah registered that fact with mild surprise as he leaped out of the car and ran for the lobby.

The lobby was large and open on the far end. Jeremiah scanned the area quickly and then made his way to the elevators. He had no way of knowing if Marge would actually be in her room, but that's where Al was heading. Jeremiah just hoped he wasn't too late to save her or catch him.

When the elevator let him off he headed in the direction of her room, moving fast, but with heightened caution. Al was armed and a desperate man with a gun was always a dangerous, unpredictable man.

When he found the room, he paused for a moment, listening. He didn't hear anything and he finally reached out and knocked on the door, making sure to stand well to one side. A few moments later it was opened by a large, amiable looking woman who blinked at him in curiosity.

"Ma'am, my name is Jeremiah. I was wondering if I could ask you a few questions about the accident you had the other day with the life preserver," he said, staring over her shoulder and trying to get a look into the room. The way the room was angled, though, he could only see part of it.

"Oh, of course, such wonderful timing," she said, standing back to let him enter.

"Why is that?" he asked, walking forward, senses alert.

"A gentleman from the crew who was there that day is here right now. I'm sure he could help answer your questions, too."

She turned and led the way into the room. A man was standing by the table, a bouquet of flowers in his hand. He looked at Jeremiah, his posture tense, alert, sizing the rabbi up even as Jeremiah was sizing him up.

"What a coincidence," Jeremiah said.

"It's rather amazing. Al just got here."

"Hello, Al," Jeremiah said, struggling not to tip his hand while Marge was standing between them.

Al dipped his head briefly in acknowledgement.

"I'm surprised to see you here," Jeremiah said.

Al shrugged. "I felt bad that I couldn't visit her in the hospital. After all, I was the one who gave her the life preserver. I still can't figure out what could have been wrong with it to make it sink like that. Bad luck."

"He brought me these beautiful flowers," Marge said, beaming from ear-to-ear.

"That was nice of him," Jeremiah said.

"It was the least I could do," Al said. "Besides, it's not good for business when a tourist gets hurt."

There was something about the way that he said 'tourist' that caught Jeremiah's attention. There was a certain level of vehemence, resentment almost bordering on hatred when he used the word.

"Well, I certainly had the tar scared out of me, but I wasn't hurt, not really," Marge said. "Honestly, I wish everyone would stop fussing."

Jeremiah shrugged. "We just want to make sure nothing like that happens again."

"I think we can all agree about that," Al said.

Jeremiah stood there. Was it possible he had misinterpreted the reason for Al's visit to Marge? It seemed unlikely. He still hadn't been able to pin him to the smugglers beyond a shadow of a doubt. But that kind of proof was required by police and attorneys and jurists. Jeremiah was none of those, but he was more than willing to be Al's executioner.

He stared hard at Al. Al just looked at him with wide, curious eyes. He was a good actor, that much Jeremiah had to give him.

"So, what can I do for you, young man?" Marge asked Jeremiah.

Jeremiah answered, but kept his eyes on Al. "I'm here to ask you a few questions about your accident."

"Oh, but I already told everyone at the hospital, and answered questions for that nice representative from the cruise company. I simply don't know how that life preserver could have failed like that."

"I'm not so much interested in the life preserver as I am something else."

"Oh?"

"I'm trying to find out what happened to another passenger on the cruise. Cindy Preston."

And at the mention of her name, Al turned a shade paler. Jeremiah lunged forward even as Al pulled his gun.

He knocked the gun from the other man's hand and it went arcing through the air. He heard Marge scream, but he didn't have time to deal with her as he lunged forward and grabbed Al by the throat. He swept the man's legs out from under him and followed him down to the ground, putting his knee into Al's sternum with enough force that he heard a rib crack.

Marge was still screaming and out of the corner of his eye he saw her move toward the phone. The last thing he needed was security or the police arriving before he'd found out what he needed to know.

He turned his head just slightly. "Sit!" he barked at her.

She froze like a deer in the headlights, staring at him in terror.

"This man came here to kill you so that you couldn't talk to anyone anymore about that damaged life preserver," he said. "Now, sit down and be quiet while I get some answers from him."

Marge gasped and sank down on the edge of the bed. Satisfied that she would stay there, at least for a while, Jeremiah turned his attention back to Al.

"Where is Cindy?" he demanded.

"I don't know!" Al sputtered.

"Try again," Jeremiah said, putting more pressure on the man's chest.

"How should I know? I don't even know her last name!"

"Did she see you, is that why you tried to kill her?"

"Yes, I had to. She was going to ruin everything," Al said. "I rigged the life preserver."

"And when you failed to kill her what happened next?" Jeremiah asked.

"I freaked out. I was afraid someone would figure out what I had done."

"And that's why you came to kill Marge?"

Al nodded frantically. "I didn't want to, but she's just a stupid haole and the cause is bigger than her, bigger than me."

"And what about Cindy?"

"I don't know! I don't know where she went."

"She was kidnapped by your cohorts."

Al shook his head fiercely. "No one knew about her. I didn't tell. I figured she was a stupid tourist, didn't know anything, but when she recognized me on that boat from the night before —"

"The night before?" Jeremiah demanded, shaking Al hard.

Al nodded frantically.

"Where exactly did she see you?" Jeremiah demanded.

"On the north shore, at the resort site. She could have ruined everything."

Jeremiah's mind was whirling. Cindy hadn't seen this guy retrieving drugs from the water at Pearl Harbor. She'd seen him hours later on the opposite side of the island, but doing what? Cause, he'd mentioned a cause.

"Tell me exactly what she saw you doing," Jeremiah demanded.

"She saw us planting the bodies. When she saw me on the ship the next morning she said she thought I was an archaeologist. I told her lots of people had two jobs and we help out where we could. I panicked, okay? This is bigger than just me."

Jeremiah was even more confused than he had been a moment before. "So, she saw you planting the bodies at the resort site?" he asked, struggling to figure out what exactly that meant without showing his own ignorance on the subject and risking Al clamping down.

He took a stab in the dark. "So, you tried to kill her. Did you kill Uncle as well?"

Tears sprang into Al's eyes. "That wasn't me, man. That was Kimo. I begged him not to. Uncle was one of our biggest supporters. He contributed so much money to the cause."

"What cause?" Jeremiah asked.

And then he could see the dawning light in Al's eyes as the other realized that Jeremiah knew far less than he thought and maybe he should shut up fast. Jeremiah didn't want to give him a chance to make that choice.

He slammed Al's head hard against the floor. The smell of blood filled the air as the skin on the man's scalp split.

"Stop, please!" Al begged.

"The pain stops only when you've told me everything I want to know."

Jeremiah threw a sharp glance at Marge who had started to edge toward the telephone. "Stay put," he hissed.

She nodded and seemed to curl in on herself.

"Hawaii for Hawaiians," Al said. "The tourists are ruining the islands and we had to protect them, particularly the north shore. We had to stop them from creating that new resort. Uncle contributed a lot of money, trying to get it shut down legally and then funding us as we sabotaged the project."

"So, what went wrong?"

"Nothing worked. Then Kimo had a great idea. His cousin's brother-in-law works for one of the archaeology firms on the island. He knew that if enough bodies were found on the property they'd have to shut the project down, that the ground would be sacred."

"I've been hearing about that on the

radio," Marge interjected suddenly. "Everyone seems very upset."

"So, you couldn't find enough bodies on the site and you started planting bodies?" Jeremiah asked, beginning to put the pieces together.

"Yeah, but they have to be like, old. So we did some research and then we dug them up from some different places around the island and we've been burying them there. It was perfect. But then Uncle found out and he went all pupule, telling us we had desecrated the bodies, that it was disrespectful. We told him we would put them back once it was over, but he was furious. He was going to tell the authorities. He was going to ruin everything we had worked for."

"So Kimo killed him."

"Yes. The cause is bigger than anyone, than everyone," Al said.

"And Cindy saw you moving some of those bodies?"

"Yes. Then when she recognized me . . ." Al drifted off.

"And you have no idea who kidnapped her? Could it be Kimo?"

Al's eyes bulged. "She's been kidnapped?"

Jeremiah nodded.

"I didn't know. And I never told Kimo or

any of the others about her. They couldn't know."

"I found drugs and money stashed in your kitchen," Jeremiah said.

"Oh man, that's the last of the money Uncle gave us. He gave Kimo drugs, too. I tell him they're no good, but he never believes me."

"So you don't know anything about the drug trade around Pearl Harbor?"

Al shook his head and there was truth in his eyes.

Jeremiah felt like he had landed back at square one. He had found Cindy's would be killer, but he still had no clue who could have kidnapped her. Anger flashed through him white hot and it was all he could do not to snap Al's neck for having tried to kill Cindy.

Instead he stood to his feet and turned to Marge. "Don't worry, I'm calling the cops."

He dialed Kapono. "You all patched up?"

"Just getting out of the emergency room now. I told them they couldn't hold me. What do you have?"

"The name of Uncle's killer and a conspirator in a massive grave robbing and sabotage ring on the north shore."

There was silence for a moment and then Kapono said something in Hawaiian. "You don't mess around, do you?"

"No."

"You're just like her. You're on the island a day and you find more trouble than most do in a lifetime."

"What can I say? It's a gift."

"Did he say where they were keeping Cindy?"

"That's the bad news. These guys aren't the ones that took her."

There was more Hawaiian on the other end of the line. "Okay tell me where you are," Kapono finally asked.

Jeremiah gave him the hotel and room number.

"I'll be there in fifteen. And I've got something for you that just came in."

"What's that?"

"The name of the taxi driver we've been looking for."

An hour later as the seas swelled around the boat she was in Cindy was regretting her decision. Her stomach was roiling, but at least this time she was tied up on deck and not down below. Once they had been out of sight of land Mr. Black had allowed her to come up and take in some of the sea air as he put it.

She still had no clue what island she had

been on and when she asked he refused to tell her. She just prayed that when they made it to Oahu she found a way to keep stalling him. She didn't know just how long she could keep up the charade of being the courier and that she had hidden whatever it was that he was looking for.

Again she went over everything she had seen in Uncle's restaurant, trying to figure out what it could be that he wanted. It was possible whoever killed Uncle had taken it or that the police had bagged it as some sort of evidence. There were too many things she didn't know or understand to help her continue to lie to him effectively.

He was standing, leaning against the rail, a mai tai in his hand, looking for all the world like a rich playboy instead of a psychopathic criminal.

"Did you kill Uncle?" she asked suddenly, surprising herself.

He turned and looked at her. "You don't know who killed Uncle?" he asked.

"No," she said, hoping it was okay to admit that.

"Then that's something we have in common. However, I'd very much like to know. I don't appreciate people killing my colleagues without my leave."

"Do you think it was random?" she asked.

He snorted. "No more than you do. No, it was a targeted attack. Idiots probably hoped to put a dent in my business. Although, I long suspected I wasn't the only one in the islands that Uncle was working for."

She remembered what Kapono had told her about his suspicions. "You think he was laundering money for someone else, too?"

"It stands to reason."

"Then maybe one of them killed him."

"It's possible. Uncle might have crossed one of his other business partners, but I don't think so. He was a crook, but he was always straight in his dealings with me. He could have retired a very wealthy man if he wanted to. All he had to do was keep playing straight with everyone for a couple of more years."

"You actually believe in honor among thieves?" she asked.

He smiled, a chilling sight. "Thieves? No. Businessmen? Yes. Uncle never took anything that didn't belong to him, at least not that I know. He provided a service to select people who needed it and charged a fee for that service. A fee I happily paid for fifteen years."

"He didn't seem like a rich man," Cindy ventured. At the very least if his restaurant was his front she would have thought he would have put a little more into it. Then again, maybe he lived in a fancy house or kept his wealth well-hidden.

Mr. Black shrugged. "I don't know what he did with his money. That was business. All I care about is what he did with my money." He gave her a hard look. "And that's *our* business."

Cindy wasn't sure how much further to push her luck in discussing all this with Mr. Black. How many questions could she ask before he began to suspect that she had been telling the truth in the beginning, that she really did have no idea what he was looking for or where it was?

He was laundering money through Uncle's restaurant. Think, what could it be that he actually wanted from Uncle?

She wracked her brain. Money was an obvious answer. She remembered the cash in the cash register and the money in the tip jar. Maybe the killer hadn't bothered because it was small change compared to what he was after. But would Uncle really have had stacks of cash sitting around waiting to give to Mr. Black or one of his lackeys? It seemed unlikely to her. On television drug dealers always did deals in cash. But this was real life, and, as Mr. Black had put it, a business transaction, hid-ing the true source of the income. Maybe it wasn't done the same way.

Maybe it was done by checks or money orders. There were lots of ways for people to transfer money without having to use briefcases of cash like in some gangster film. Maybe they used one of those methods. They could even have made the transfer by credit card for all she knew.

She blinked as a thought hit her. *Or by wire transfers.*

And that's when she remembered the business card that the taxi driver had given her. The one that he had told her to show to Uncle. The one that didn't look exactly like a normal business card but had a long series of numbers on it. She gasped as she realized Mr. Black was right. She had been in possession of what he wanted even though she wasn't any longer.

But she knew who was. She squeezed her eyes shut. How was she going to convince Mr. Black that the information he wanted was in a police station?

"Something wrong?" she heard him ask.

"I'm getting more seasick, and I think I'm going to throw up," she said. It was at least partially true.

15

True to his word, Kapono arrived in fifteen minutes. To Jeremiah, though, it seemed like an eternity while he waited to hear who the taxi driver was that had sent Cindy to Uncle's. Marge and Al were both visibly relieved when the detective showed up.

Kapono had clearly come straight from the hospital. In lieu of one shirt sleeve he had white bandages wrapped around his arm. He listened slack-jawed as Jeremiah explained everything to him. During several points in the narrative Marge nodded enthusiastically while Al just sat groaning on the floor.

"You've got to be kidding me," the big detective finally said.

Jeremiah shook his head grimly.

"There's going to be the devil to pay sorting out all those remains. I don't envy whoever has to deal with the Burial Council on that one."

"It's terrible and I'm sure it's going to be a mess for quite a while," Jeremiah said, frustration bubbling to the surface. "But, of course, the worst part is, they have nothing to do with the kidnapping."

"Ah, but the cab driver has to," Kapono said, reaching into his shirt pocket. "My guys finished narrowing down the list of drivers it couldn't be and then we took the remaining drivers and compared them to the description Cindy gave me. Everything points to one guy, named Manny."

"Let me guess, he hasn't shown up to work today?"

"No, he's working. Best part is, he's got a fare he's driving in from the north shore as we speak and he has no idea we're looking for him. His dispatcher is really helping us out with this one."

"Great, so let's go grab him when he drops off his passenger."

Kapono glanced away.

"What's wrong?" Jeremiah asked sharply.

"We've talked to a couple of guys who have dealt with him before. They're under the impression that Manny won't talk for anything."

"He will if I break his legs," Jeremiah growled.

"Which, officially, I can't let you do,"

Kapono said.

Jeremiah stared hard at the detective who steadfastly was refusing to meet his eyes.

Just then a couple of uniformed officers entered the room. Kapono waved them over and pointed to Al. "Make sure and read him his rights while I go take some more statements."

As the officers were taking charge of Al, Kapono grabbed Jeremiah's arm and steered him toward the door. Outside in the hall they moved toward the elevators until they were well out of earshot of the room. Finally Kapono stopped, but Jeremiah noticed he still wouldn't look him in the eyes.

"You know, Cindy is a nice wahine."

"Very nice," Jeremiah agreed. "Borders on a saint in my book."

"And we're well outside the range of time where kidnapping victims have a chance of coming back home."

"I know."

Kapono pulled a small disc out of his pocket and handed it to Jeremiah. "Just do me a favor and wear this tracker so that we can find you."

Without saying anything Jeremiah bent down, pulled up his left pant leg, and stuffed the tracker down inside his sock and

into the top of the shoe. When he straight-
ened back up Kapono was nodding ap-
proval.

Next Kapono handed Jeremiah a slip of
paper.

"We're going to be taking him down when
he reaches this location. Now, for your own
safety, I don't want to see you anywhere
near the place. You should go home and wait
for a phone call. You understand?"

"Perfectly," Jeremiah said.

"You know, I should put your okole back
on a plane right now."

"You couldn't," Jeremiah said simply.

"Yeah, I know, but I feel like I should at
least try."

He could see the struggle Kapono was going through. Every instinct he had as a cop
was to get Jeremiah out of the equation
because he was a civilian and a loose can-
non.

"It would be a waste of everyone's time if
you did, especially when we have more
important things to worry about," Jeremiah
said, and he reached out and very deliberately patted Kapono on the arm, exactly
where he'd gotten shot, just hard enough to
make the detective wince.

"Remember, I don't want to see you
anywhere near there," Kapono said, taking

a step back out of arm's reach.

"Don't worry," Jeremiah said. "You won't."

Mark's eyes were blurring as he stared at the computer screen. He'd exhausted every last lead he could think of and no one would agree to talk to him. He was beginning to think that he would never know the truth about his former partner.

The phone rang and he answered. "Hello?"

"Mark, it's William over here in Hawaii."

"Any word on Cindy yet?" Mark asked, his stomach twisting itself into a knot as he heard his friend's voice.

"Nothing yet, we're still tracking down leads."

There was a pause . . . too long, and Mark began to wonder why William had really called. "What's going on?" he finally asked.

"I was just wondering, how well do you know the rabbi?"

Mark turned away from his computer and his eyes fell on a picture of him and Paul. "I guess as well as anyone can know anyone else," he said softly.

"Sorry, I didn't hear you."

"Oh, yeah, I've known him for just over a year. He's a good guy. He plays things a bit close to the vest, but he's a real white knight. Why do you ask?"

There was another lengthy pause.

"William? Something hasn't happened to him, has it?"

"To him? No. But he's been here less than twenty-four hours and he's already helped expose a drug trafficking ring, identified a killer and caught his co-conspirator in a scandal that's going to rock this island for some time, and gotten one of my best detectives shot in the shoulder."

And for some reason Mark couldn't help but smile. "What can I say? He's not going to leave any stone unturned until he finds Cindy. And heaven help whoever's standing in his way."

"I'm beginning to get that idea. Is he this much trouble at home?"

"Worse," Mark said.

"Well, one of these days I'm going to have to repay this . . . favor."

"Oh, what did you have in mind?" Mark asked.

"I've got a writer who lives out here, in one of the hotels as a matter of fact, who I'm going to encourage to take a trip to your neck of the woods. Maybe send her to The Zone theme park, take in the sights."

"See if she stumbles across a dead body

in my jurisdiction?" Mark guessed.

"Glad to see you're still clever as ever."

"Uh huh. Tell you what, you send me back Cindy and Jeremiah in one piece, and you can send whoever you want out here on vacation."

There was a deep chuckle on the other end of the line. "I'm going to hold you to that."

"I know you will."

Cindy was sitting in the bowels of the ship. Mr. Black had had one of his goons escort her down there. She hoped that meant they were getting close to land. She was beyond ready to get off the boat for her stomach's sake, even if that was going to bring a reckoning she wasn't ready for. She thought that if she made it through this whole ordeal she might never go on another boat again. After all, even the pleasure trip had turned out to be a disaster. She shuddered as she again realized that it could have been her with the life preserver had she actually overcome her fear of the water and gone in.

He meant for it to be me.

She thought about Al. Why on earth would he want to kill her? She had done nothing to him and there was nothing she could think of that connected him to Mr.

Black or Uncle.

And then she remembered him and the two other guys on that building site on the north shore. She relived the entire encounter in her mind, desperate to take her focus off the fact that she wanted to vomit.

She thought about the kayak pulled up on the beach. The two men had been carrying the bones away from the kayak and toward the holes in the earth. That made no sense at all. If they were using the kayak for transportation for some reason why wouldn't they be putting the bodies in it instead?

She'd assumed they hadn't wanted to drive vehicles onto the site, possibly causing more destruction, hence the kayak, but something was wrong with that picture. Had they been dumping a fresh body into an old grave site?

She closed her eyes as she continued to struggle against the nausea. She thought of the arguments she'd heard about the resort site over the radio in the car, the way the taxi driver had seemed like he didn't want the resort to go forward just like some of the other locals.

If they were trying to hide a body, some-place teeming with archaeologists would be the last place they should go. No, she was sure they weren't that stupid. The body would be sure to be found.

They must have wanted the body to be found.

And it came to her swiftly. What if they had been digging up bodies and reburying them there for the sole purpose of shutting down the construction? And if they thought she had seen them, figured out what they were up to . . .

"They would try to kill me," she whispered out loud. "Otherwise all their schemes would be over."

She felt the boat turn and she prayed that meant they were almost in port. Then she began praying just as fervently that she'd figure out how to stall Mr. Black once they got there.

She wasn't sure, but it felt like they were slowing down. That had to mean they were entering port. This might be her last chance to escape.

Jeremiah kept his promise to Kapono. The detective didn't see him as Jeremiah concealed himself behind some shrubbery and flower beds at the entrance to the restaurant Manny the taxi driver was supposed to be arriving at soon with guests.

Jeremiah had changed out of his all black

clothes into tourist casual shorts and an aloha shirt, which ironically was helping him blend in with the flower beds. He had still beat the police to the restaurant by five minutes. In his shirt pocket he had a thick, metal penlight.

He watched as they deployed around the perimeter, struggling to blend in. If Manny was smart and paying attention he'd see them in a heartbeat. Hopefully he was distracted. Jeremiah didn't want to miss his shot at him. Nor did he want to risk the lives of the passengers Manny was driving.

A couple of taxis pulled up, but none of them were Wiki Taxis. From where he was he couldn't see as much of the drive as he wanted so he kept glancing at Kapono's face. The detective still was minus a sleeve on his shirt and his white bandage stood out in stark contrast to his deeply tanned skin.

Finally, he saw Kapono stiffen. A moment later a car slid into view. It was a Wiki Taxi. He saw another police officer take a step forward, hand on the gun he wasn't concealing very well. From where he was Jeremiah couldn't see the driver, but from the body language of everyone he could see this was definitely the right cab.

As it slid to a stop in front of the door

Jeremiah stepped out from behind the bushes, making sure to keep his back to Kapono. He took three quick strides forward and pulled open the door, startling the people inside.

"Sorry, sir, ma'am, I've got to get to the hospital," he said, putting a sense of urgency in his voice.

It worked, they threw a couple of bills toward the driver and got out quickly. Jeremiah slid in, slammed the door, and said, "An extra hundred if you get me there in ten minutes."

The driver stepped on the gas and the car went shooting back out toward the street. Jeremiah saw one undercover officer jump backward in surprise as they almost plowed him over.

"What's the trouble?" the driver asked.

Jeremiah looked at the license hanging on the dash. Manny.

"It's my wife. Something's happened to her. Hurry please."

"That's awful," Manny said.

He took a turn fast and then another. Hopefully it would be enough to buy them a couple of minutes while the police tried to figure out where they were headed.

"Yes, it really is," Jeremiah said. "I can't believe this happened to us, and on vacation, too."

"The world can be cruel sometimes."

Manny took two more turns. He really was racing to get the money. Jeremiah removed the metal penlight from his pocket and held it in his hand.

"What happened to your wife?" Manny asked.

Jeremiah pushed the penlight into the back of Manny's thick neck. The driver jerked, startled, and swerved into oncoming traffic, but quickly righted himself and slowed the car down.

"She was kidnapped," Jeremiah said softly.

The boat was in dock and Cindy's stomach had calmed only slightly when Mr. Black made his appearance. He was smiling, and, if anything, it only made him look more evil, like some kind of slippery snake that was about to devour her as though she were a helpless mouse.

She set her jaw. She refused to be anyone's mouse. There had to be a way out, she just had to figure out what it was. He came to a stop in front of her and stared at her long and hard. The section of the ship that she was in was dark and windowless, and from the looks of it, was probably supposed to be used for cargo.

She took a deep breath. Instead of waiting for him to start asking her questions she decided to go on the offensive. "Does Al work for you?" she asked.

"Who's Al?" he asked.

She gave a brief description of him. "He works on one of the snorkeling tour boats."

Mr. Black shook his head, but even in the dim light coming from the doorway she could see the curiosity in his eyes. "Why do you ask?"

"He tried to kill me when I was on one of those boats the same day that you're goon kidnapped me."

Mr. Black looked genuinely surprised and actually a trifle concerned. "Why, did he know what you had of mine?"

Cindy stared at him for a moment, praying that the next words out of her mouth would be the right ones.

"I'm not sure what he thought or what he knew or who he was working for. What I do know is that he wanted me dead, but he was being cautious, wanted to make it look like an accident."

"And what did you do to him in return?"

"Nothing. I didn't realize exactly what was going on until later. I do know, though, that I had seen him the night before up on the north shore."

Mr. Black swore under his breath and added a name to it which Cindy didn't recognize. She hoped it was one of his enemies or competitors. Anything to get him thinking about someone else other than her while she continued to work at the knots that bound her hands behind her back.

"I mean, the only reason you even knew to look for me was because of the taxi driver, right?"

"Right, right," he said, his voice distant. He was drumming his fingers against his chin.

"So, what changed between seven p.m. Saturday and eight a.m. Sunday that put me on this guy's radar."

Mr. Black began to pace. He cast an occasional sideways glance at her. Then he turned abruptly and left the room, leaving the door open behind him.

Cindy sagged briefly in relief, but kept working her fingers on the rope. She had no way of knowing how long the reprieve would last but she had to assume it would only be a matter of minutes. She had no idea what he was going to do or who he was going to call, but hopefully whatever the result was it would buy her the time she needed.

■ ■ ■ ■

"What you want with me?" Manny asked, terror filling his voice.

Jeremiah jabbed the penlight harder into the back of his neck. "I want you to take me to wherever it is she's being held or I'm going to blow your brains all across that dashboard."

"No way! You'd be killed, too."

"My wife's been kidnapped. Ask me if I care terribly much about my own safety at the moment. Besides, your car has rear airbags. I'll survive a crash. You, on the other hand, won't."

"Please, I don't know what you're talking about! I never kidnapped anybody."

"But you know who did."

"No, you got me mistaken for somebody else."

"No, Manny. You're the one who picked up Cindy at her hotel Saturday morning, drove her to Pearl Harbor, insisted she try eating at Uncle's, and gave her a card with a bank account number on it to give him."

Manny gasped. "I no do anything to her."

"No, but someone killed Uncle. She was never able to give him the card. And you told somebody about it, somebody who wanted that card. Somebody who was willing to do anything it took to get it."

"Please, I didn't mean for them to kidnap her. Maybe just snatch her purse or something."

"Okay, if you didn't mean it, prove it."

"How?"

"Take me to wherever she's being held."

"I don't know, you gotta believe me."

"No, what I gotta do is get the information I want out of you or kill you. Your choice, of course."

Jeremiah jabbed the penlight harder into Manny's neck, knowing there was no way the man would be able to tell that it wasn't a gun.

"Please, I can help you. I'm Manny, I'm the go to guy. I can get you anything you want on this island."

"What I want is Cindy back. Right now. Can you help me with that or not?"

There was a long pause and then Manny nodded his head. "Yes, I think I can."

"Good."

"There's a warehouse the boss has. It's where he conducts business. Good business and bad business. That's where she would be."

"And how do I know you're not lying?"

"How do I know you're not going to kill

me anyway when we get there?"

"I'll make you a promise, Manny. I find her, alive, and you get to live. If I don't find her alive, I'll kill you."

"But what if they killed her already?"

"Then you'll just have to pray to whatever deity will listen to you that they haven't. Understood?"

Manny nodded jerkily. "That's fair."

"How far is this warehouse?"

"About another twenty minutes."

"You were making such good time earlier. What do you say we cut that time in half. I don't want the police to find us before we get there."

Manny made a groaning sound deep in his throat as he probably realized that even if he did live life was about to change for him dramatically. Accessory to kidnapping could do that to a person.

Manny floored the gas again and the car sped forward. Jeremiah gritted his teeth and waited, muscles coiled. Adrenalin was rushing through him. The trick was to control it and not be controlled by it. He tracked every turn they made so he could replicate them if he had to.

And finally they made it into a warehouse district. Manny swerved into an alley, car bouncing up and down hard as it hit a couple of potholes. He drove halfway down it then slammed on the brakes and pointed to a side door into one of the buildings.

"She in there, I swear it."

Jeremiah leaned forward and slammed the man's head into the steering wheel, knocking him out. He got out of the car cautiously, looking around. He pocketed his penlight as his eyes continued to sweep the area. He didn't see anyone, though, and he finally moved closer to the door.

He tried to imagine what he was going to find inside. He should have made the driver tell him before he knocked him out. How many people were inside, whether Cindy was being held in the main room or a separate room, the kind of weapons present. All of these would have been invaluable to know.

He wished he had a weapon of any kind, but sometimes a person could rely too much on a weapon and it could do more harm than good. He'd just have to go slow, be careful. He eased back away from the door. There might be another way in, something less obvious, something that wouldn't announce his presence so quickly.

He took a few steps back and looked up at the building. There were a few windows high up, but no fire escapes or scaffolding.

He'd have to go into one from the roof, but that was predicated on his being able to get to the roof. He walked quickly to the back of the building, aware that every second he delayed could be disastrous. But so could storming right into a nest of vipers. Around the back of the building he didn't see anything that looked more promising.

He made a decision not to lap the rest of the building. It would take too much time. He just had to take his chances with the door Manny had shown him. He returned to the door and put his ear against it, straining to hear anything coming from inside.

All was silent, though. Finally, he put his hand on the door handle.

Suddenly, he froze. Something wasn't right. He tilted his head. Was that the sound of a footstep? He let go of the handle and slowly turned around.

Three guys in their twenties stood scattered in the alley, each with a gun trained on him, each well out of reach.

"Can I help you guys?" Jeremiah asked.

"Manny here does not drive his taxi into the alley unless he has a problem he needs taken care of," one of them spoke up.

Jeremiah glanced up and belatedly saw the tiny, half-concealed security camera that was trained on the entrance to the alleyway.

There was no use in bluffing. Two seconds would show them that Manny was unconscious.

There was nothing within his reach that could be used as a weapon. He turned his eyes back to the one who seemed to be in charge.

"What are you doing here?" the man demanded.

There was only one thing to do. Jeremiah had to allow himself to be captured. Nothing in him liked that plan, but he didn't see how he had a choice at this point. In order to get out of this alive he would have to kill all three men before one of them could kill him. If he survived he still wouldn't know where to go to find Cindy. On the other hand, if they took him hostage, they might take him to wherever Cindy was being held. "Please," he said, raising his hands into the air. "I'm just trying to find Cindy Preston."

"Why you want find her so bad?" one of the guys asked.

Jeremiah blinked. They were holding Cindy because they wanted something from her, something they thought she could get them but was reluctant to. He needed to make himself a bargaining chip that they thought they could use to get her to talk. He only hoped that whatever condition she

273

was in Cindy would be able to figure out what was happening and play along.

"Because I'm her husband," he said.

They all stared at him for a moment and then the one said, "Put him in the car." He then pulled out a cell phone.

Cindy heard Mr. Black's footsteps on the stairs outside the room a moment before he came in. She wanted to scream in frustration. She had been hoping for more time.

"So, I made a couple of quick phone calls, but I didn't have to make many. It turns out the driver, Manny, just made an unscheduled stop and my men are going to check it out and ask him some questions."

Her heart thundered. What would he tell them? Surely the truth, that she was just an innocent tourist who had no way of knowing what it was that he had given her. She could feel her shoulders bunching as she strained at her restraints.

Move, now, now, now! she was screaming at herself.

Mr. Black's phone rang. "That should be them right on schedule."

He listened for a moment and then he began to chuckle. The sound sent chills up her spine and she couldn't help but feel that whatever had happened it was very bad news for her. After a minute he hung up.

"Well, it turns out they're going to have to wait a few minutes to talk to Manny. He was knocked out cold."

"Oh?" she said, still not sure why he was chuckling.

"But my men did find one very interesting thing. Or rather, one very interesting *person*."

"I don't understand," she said.

His grin broadened. "We just captured your husband."

16

Cindy stared at him in shock. Husband? Before she could open her mouth to say that she wasn't married, she forced herself to stop and think. Who would make such a claim and why?

The answer was so simple. Jeremiah, they had to be talking about Jeremiah. She could think of no one else who would possibly make such an outrageous claim. What was he doing here though? He had to be there to find her, rescue her. But now, apparently, he had been captured. That meant he was in as much danger as she was. She suddenly felt like she was going to be sick all over again. Her head swam, and before she quite knew what was happening she said, "I don't believe you, show him to me."

Mr. Black chuckled. "You'll see him soon enough. And when you do, you'll have five minutes to tell me everything I want to know before I kill him."

"No! You can't do that!"

"Your choice," he said. "I'll leave you to think about that," he said as he left the room, shutting the door behind him.

She was in total darkness. Her emotions were yo-yoing between hope and despair, joy and terror. Jeremiah had come for her, he had come to find her. Maybe he was working with the police. Her thoughts flashed to Kapono and she could feel her cheeks growing hot. Was it even possible that she was thinking about how embarrassed she'd be if the two of them met?

Her heart was racing even as her mind was going a million miles a minute. Had Jeremiah really come to find her himself? She couldn't imagine a police officer saying something like that. And it was an old joke between her and Jeremiah harkening back to the time the serial killer had put her in the hospital and only family had been allowed to visit.

But why would he have risked everything to come find her? In the next breath she thought about her crazy drive up to Green Pastures camp to try and save him and she understood. This was what you did when you cared for someone. You risked it all to help them. Would she have been content to sit back and do nothing if he was the one who vanished.

No! everything in her seemed to cry out. Maybe the old her would have, but not the new her, not the her that knew Jeremiah.

She felt a lump in her throat even as she tried to force herself to calm down. Whatever happened next she was going to need to be alert, ready to make a move the moment she could to try and help them both escape. She just prayed that Jeremiah had a plan.

She renewed her struggles against the ropes that bound her. In her fervor she briefly considered trying to break or dislocate her thumb. She'd heard that helped with handcuffs, but she didn't know if she could make it work with the ropes with the way they were crisscrossed. And she was going to need to be as clear-headed as possible very, very quickly.

She kept working at them, though, until her fingers were raw and bleeding from the constant chafing and contact with the rough rope. Jeremiah was coming. He was on his way. That's what Mr. Black had said. And she needed to be ready when he got there.

Riding in the backseat of the car between the two thugs Jeremiah was sorely tempted to try and escape. He forced himself to breathe, though, reminding himself that this was his best shot at actually finding Cindy. He thought of the tracking chip inside his sock and hoped that Kapono and other officers wouldn't be far behind when he did find her. He was glad now that he had agreed to wear it even though it went against every instinct he had.

The drive seemed to take forever. The mere fact that they hadn't knocked him out or blindfolded him attested to the fact that they had no intention of letting him live. The same would almost certainly be true of Cindy.

The best he could do was watch and be patient. When the time came to make a move it would have to be done swiftly with no mistakes. Both their lives depended on it.

When at last they were pulling into a parking spot near a dock he thought of the entry Uncle had had in his books about the big boat man. Sure enough at the end of the pier he could see a yacht bouncing up and down on the waves.

The guy on his left stuck a gun into his side. "You move, you say a word and you get it and so does your old lady."

For all that Jeremiah was sure the guy was serious, he was also an amateur. The way he had the gun angled a bullet would miss all the major organs. Again Jeremiah had to remind himself of his purpose and not just take the gun away from the man and beat him with it.

For all he knew Cindy wasn't on the boat and they were going to have to sail a distance to get to her. Plus, there was an awful lot of ground to cover between the car and the ship and even if he went into the water if there was any kind of lookout they'd become suspicious quickly that no one was coming from the car.

So he forced himself to nod and tried to look frightened and submissive. At least the frightened part was true, not for himself, but for Cindy.

All three of the thugs had piled into the car with him, leaving Manny still unconscious in his taxi. That was the one thing going in his favor. None of them knew that he could be dangerous when pushed and Manny would have been happy to swear to that. He also still had the penlight in his pocket. There were a couple of ways he could use it as a weapon if he really had to.

They got out of the car and a few steps later they were walking down the pier. The leader led the way and the other two each had hold of one of Jeremiah's arms. He grit his teeth in frustration. It would have been so simple to knock them both into the water, take a quick step, and snatch the gun from the waistband of the guy in front of him.

Again, though, he had to force himself to remain calm and to not act on his impulses. This wasn't about his freedom. It was about Cindy's.

He could hear the creak of each wooden plank beneath their feet, the lapping of the ocean waves, the trill of a bird. All his senses were growing sharper. Soon he would have need of all of them. There was only one way this was going to end, one way it could end.

And he tried not to think about what would happen afterward when he and Cindy made it back to California and she could no longer look him in the eyes without seeing a monster.

The boat was getting nearer. Twenty feet.

He was going to make all of them pay for taking Cindy. Fifteen feet.

He was going to personally hunt down anybody who had been involved with her kidnapping in any way. Ten feet.

And he was going to blaze her name across the island so that everyone would know that she was not to be touched. Five feet.

And then he would tell her the truth.

Cindy felt the rope give way. She twisted and wriggled her right wrist until she was free. She dug her fingernails harder into the knots still binding her left hand to the back of the chair. Her fingernails were tearing and bleeding and it felt like they were on fire. Her hand was shaking from the exertion and cramping from the dehydration. And above her on deck she heard the sound of many footsteps, walking.

Jeremiah stepped onto the boat and it was all he could do to remind himself to play the part of frantic, concerned husband. *Harmless*, frantic, concerned husband, he amended.

A man was standing in front of him, white shirt opened at the neck, a pair of Dockers on. "So, the little wildcat has a husband."

Rage roared through Jeremiah and it passed leaving him shaking. The adrenalin was controlling him which was bad, but he could at least use it for his act.

"Please, where is she? You haven't hurt her, have you? Look we don't have a ton of money, but whatever we have, it's yours. I just need to see her."

The man sneered. "You really think this is

about some stupid ransom?"

"Isn't it?" Jeremiah asked, letting all the fear he'd been feeling for her show in his voice.

"Your wife has something of mine and I want it back."

"I don't understand," Jeremiah said.

"No, I'm pretty sure you don't, but she does."

"Please, whatever it is, I'm sure she didn't mean to take it."

"Maybe and maybe not. It doesn't really matter. What does matter is that you're going to help me get it back from her. Right now."

The man turned and led the way toward the back of the ship and then from there down a flight of stairs. At the bottom was a door. Jeremiah could feel himself gathering together, preparing. First he needed to see how Cindy was, where she was, how she was restrained. It did him no good to find her only to have her killed before he could free her.

The man pushed open the door and shoved Jeremiah inside. His eyes quickly struggled to adjust to the dim lighting. Finally he saw Cindy, tied to a chair. She was dirty, covered in what looked to be blood, some of it fresh, and shaking. But she was alive.

He stumbled toward her and the sob that escaped his lips was real.

Cindy stared in shock. It really was Jeremiah. He was there. It hadn't been some lie or trick or anything. He'd come to rescue her. Behind him in the doorway she could see Mr. Black and three other guys.

And then Mr. Black pushed Jeremiah toward her and he was stumbling forward. His hands were shaking.

"Honey, I love you. It's going to be okay. *We're* going to be okay," he was saying the words loudly and she registered in some part of her mind that they weren't just for her benefit. He was playing the part, just like back in the hospital. But even there, kidnapped and trapped in the bottom of the ship, hearing him fake tell her he loved her sent a shiver up her spine that she couldn't ignore.

She stared at him, unable to think of a single thing to say in response.

He collapsed on his knees in front of her and threw his arms around her. A moment later she could feel his fingers working at the knots that still bound her left wrist.

"Can you ever forgive me for being such an ass?" he wailed.

"Forgive you?" she finally managed to say, despite the fact that he was pressed close against her and she was trying to focus so she could help him with the knot.

"It's all my fault we're here. I should have let us go visit your sister in New York. We could be sitting, right now, in a theater on Broadway watching that chick musical you wanted to see. Can you ever forgive me?"

The knots were giving way and she began to sob in hope and desperation. Even if he untied her, how would they get past Mr. Black and the others?

"I do forgive you," she said.

"Next time, next time, we'll go anywhere you want, I swear. And I'll take out the trash from now on and put the toilet seat down just like you always want me to."

She felt moisture on her stomach and a moment later one of the thugs hauled Jeremiah to his feet. She stared at him in shock as he registered that there were real tears rolling down his cheeks.

And a moment later the last knot gave way. The rope fell to the ground behind her before she could think to stop it. Jeremiah saw and he elbowed the guy holding him and then twisted around so that he had his arm around the man's neck and had positioned him between them and the others.

Cindy jumped to her feet and stood right behind Jeremiah, her heart in her throat. What was he planning? Did he really think the others would let them just walk out of there? The man he was holding on to was gasping for air and flailing, but it was ineffectual.

Slowly they walked toward the door.

"Move away!" Jeremiah barked.

She held her breath, praying that they would do as he ordered.

For a moment nothing happened and then Mr. Black applauded. "Very good, wonderful performance. I'm very impressed. Maybe I had it wrong and you are the brains of the couple and not your wife."

"Back away."

"Or what?" Mr. Black asked.

"Or I kill your guy here," Jeremiah said, tightening his stranglehold.

His voice was so fierce that Cindy's breath caught. She actually believed he would do it. She turned to look at Mr. Black, waiting to see what he would do.

And what he did was laugh that hated laugh.

"Go ahead. Guys like him are a dime a dozen on this island. You kill him. We shoot both of you."

"You need us to find your account number," Jeremiah said.

Cindy gasped as she realized that she must have been right about the business card after all.

"Actually, I only need one of you. And since you've become a problem, we'll kill you, kneecap her. She'll tell me what I want to know, eventually."

"There's no way out," Cindy heard herself whisper. There was a despair in her voice she'd never known before. Until that moment she'd hoped that it would still all somehow be okay.

Jeremiah screamed and jumped forward. He threw the guy he was holding into the others, knocking them back onto the stairs and then he slammed closed the door and threw what sounded like a bolt.

It was pitch dark again, but a moment later she felt his hand grab hers. "There's always a way out," she heard him say and he pulled her back in the direction of the chair. Her foot grazed it as they moved past. She couldn't see a thing but she could hear the screams coming from the otherside of the door.

"Where are we going?"

And then suddenly there was light as Jeremiah threw open another door that had been behind her the whole time. "I saw it earlier," he explained as he helped her out. "It will only take them a few seconds to figure out that this is where we're going."

They began to race up the stairs when suddenly the light seemed to be blotted out again. Cindy looked up and saw the biggest man she'd ever seen in her entire life standing at the top of the stairs wearing nothing but a pair of shorts.

Jeremiah stared intently at the man blocking their way. He was willing to bet just about anything from the man's sheer size that he was Samoan. There would be no going around him, only through him.

Jeremiah reached for the penlight in his pocket, planning the moves he was going to use to take the giant down. He was going to have to kill him. He heard a crash behind him but he kept his focus on the Samoan. His hand tightened around the penlight. He saw the fight playing out in his head.

He saw himself winning.

He took a step upward and then hesitated. He didn't want Cindy to see him kill someone. Behind him he heard Cindy scream and he spun around. Mr. Black had her, a knife to her throat.

"Tell me where the numbers are!" he screamed.

"The police —"

and that was all Jeremiah got out because something hit him hard in the head and the world went black.

Jeremiah woke, but forced himself to lay very still while he tried to discern where they were. They were still alive which was nothing short of a miracle. They were also on the ocean, close to the water as he could feel the waves crash over him as the craft bounced along. He finally determined it had to be a rubber raft with a powerful outboard motor.

His wrists were bound with rope behind him, but he could tell it was a shoddy job. They didn't expect the rope to actually be able to hold him which meant that whenever they got where they were going he was as good as dead. If it hadn't been for the fact that he wasn't sure where Cindy was he would have flipped himself over the side right then.

He cursed himself for not having gone after the Samoan when he had the chance. He and Cindy could have probably escaped, but he had blown it. He had hesitated because he didn't want her to see him kill. Now, thanks to him, she might very well have to see him die.

He very slowly cracked open his eyes,

careful not to move them back and forth but only to stare straight ahead through the lashes to best avoid detection. It was still dark out but he had a feeling it wasn't that far before dawn. He could see one man sitting, his back to him, at the front of the boat. He was a huge guy, possibly the Samoan he'd heard about. If he was at the bow of the ship there had to be at least one more operating the motor at the stern.

He could feel pressure up against the back of his calves. He shifted one slightly, pushing back. There was some give. He was willing to bet it was Cindy on the floor of the raft behind him. All the more reason he couldn't jump now.

He lay still, but began slowly manipulating the ropes around his wrists. He managed to get them loose enough that he could free himself in a moment, but they would still pass a cursory inspection.

Then all that was left to do was wait. There was no way of knowing if the man behind them had a gun trained on him or if he was close enough to hurt Cindy if Jeremiah made a move.

At last the boat slowed and the way it was maneuvering it felt like they were pulling up beside something, perhaps a dock or another boat? Jeremiah risked opening his eyes just a tiny bit more and he saw a dark shadow hovering above them in the dark.

A giant ship.

"Why don't we just dump them here?" someone spoke from behind him.

The Samoan turned around. "Boss no want bodies discovered. This best way."

He heard the other man heave something off the bottom of the boat. Then the Samoan was bending over him, picking him up as though he were a ragdoll and throwing him over his shoulder.

As the big man turned Jeremiah caught a glimpse of a ladder on the side of the big ship. The first man was already climbing it with an unconscious Cindy slung over his shoulder.

The Samoan headed up next and Jeremiah forced himself to remain limp, even though it was a painful process as his legs banged against the side of the ship and the big man's shoulder dug into his ribcage.

Finally they were onboard the ship and then descending down several sets of stairs until he finally felt himself dropped unceremoniously on the ground. He forced himself not to flinch or give any sign. He heard Cindy hit the ground beside him and rage filled him. She didn't deserve to be treated like this. She didn't deserve any of it.

He cracked his eyes just a slit and he could see the legs of both men.

"So what now?" he heard the one man say.

"We kill 'em," the Samoan answered, sounding like he was cocking a gun.

"Isn't that a little moot at this point?"

"You can never be too careful, I've found."

"Okay, but let's make it quick and get out of here. This place gives me the creeps."

"You worry —"

Jeremiah kicked out, catching the Samoan in the knee. He crumpled to the ground even as Jeremiah rocketed to his feet, pulled free of his bonds, and grabbed the gun the second man was pulling from his waistband. He smashed him in the nose with it and the man staggered backward, tripping over the Samoan's body.

Jeremiah kicked the gun out of the Samoan's hand and then followed it up with another kick to the side of his knee. The man screamed in pain and the second one bounded up, running for all he was worth.

Jeremiah shot, hitting him in the shoulder on purpose. He needed him alive later to help bring the others to justice. The man staggered and then ran through an open doorway.

They were in what appeared to be the interior of a navy ship although incredibly stripped down. Alarm bells were going off in the back of his mind, but he didn't have time to stop and think about it.

"Tell me who you're working for?" he demanded of the Samoan.

The big man chuckled. "It don't matter bruddah, because we all dead."

Somewhere a warning klaxon went off. The Samoan made his move, lunging out to grab at Jeremiah's legs.

Jeremiah put a bullet in his head. As the Samoan's body fell back Jeremiah cursed to himself. The henchman was no good to him dead. He'd just have to hope he could catch up to the other one.

A groan made him spin around. Cindy was coming to.

Cindy woke slowly, blinking her overly dry eyes as fast as she could as she struggled to focus. She began to panic when all she could see was gray. Then a few seconds later she relaxed slightly as she realized that was all there was to see.

"Where are we?" she asked, testing her voice. Her throat was dry, raspy, but the words came out.

"Inside a navy ship," Jeremiah answered.

She managed to turn her head to look at him. He was standing a few feet away, tucking something into the back of his waistband and looking flustered.

"How long have we been out?" she asked.

The ropes around her wrists were chafing her but at least they hadn't cut off her blood supply.

Her eyes dropped down and she saw a body on the ground a few feet away. She jerked hard and Jeremiah raised a hand. "It's okay. He was one of the bad guys."

"Was?"

"He's dead."

"Are you sure?" she asked as he came to her side and began working on the ropes tying her wrists.

"Pretty sure," he said, his voice grim sounding.

"What is that sound?" she asked.

"Ship's alarm bells," he said as the knots began to loosen.

"What are they going to do with us?" Cindy asked as she stared around wildly.

"I think we're about to find out," Jeremiah said grimly.

Before she could ask him what he meant all around her the world exploded.

17

Cindy screamed but couldn't hear herself over the roaring of the explosions. The boat shuddered hard and lurched suddenly onto its side.

Cindy fell, skidding down what once had been the floor until she slammed up against the wall that was now the bottom part of the ship. Her entire sense of equilibrium was thrown as they were tilting. It was like being on some insane carnival ride, but there was no stopping it to get off.

"What's happening?" she screamed as Jeremiah slammed into her.

Then the roar of the explosions stopped to be replaced a moment later by the sound of rushing water.

"They're sinking the ship," Jeremiah said. "We have to get out of here now."

Around here she could hear the groaning of metal and things rattling around as though falling. She expected to be pelted by flying debris, but miraculously nothing seemed to be coming their way.

He grabbed her hands and in moments had the ropes off. Then he pulled her up to her feet. She had the unnerving sensation of going downward, like an elevator that was going a bit too fast.

"We need to get to the top of the ship," he shouted at her as he pulled her down a hallway and then angled off to the right where they encountered a ladder. Because the ship was flipped on its side, though, they didn't have to climb up it, they just kept moving, walking on the wall.

They had just made it to the next deck when water began rushing in, pooling around their feet. She screamed. Jeremiah looked at her over her shoulder.

She grabbed onto his shoulders and stood on tiptoe, trying to get as far from the water as possible even though her conscious mind knew she was crazy.

"We're going to drown!" she panted, her mind flailing wildly at the thought. This wasn't happening, couldn't be happening. She wouldn't die in the water, couldn't. It felt like the entire world was slipping away from her as panic set in. But through all the terror she could hear Jeremiah's voice loud and clear.

"Not if I can help it," he said. "Stay right behind me."

Jeremiah could feel Cindy's panic and he fought not to let it infect him as well. He pulled his penlight out of his pocket, grateful it was still there and shone it around, searching for some kind of sign or opening that would lead them to the top of the ship faster.

All the while he was searching he was thinking. It didn't seem like they had come this far getting into the belly of the ship. Maybe they'd taken the wrong passageway. It was too late for second-guessing now. They couldn't go back, all they could do was go forward and hope that G-d would lead them to where they needed to go.

He was sliding right hand along the wall that was supposed to be the ceiling of the corridor when he encountered something wet and sticky. He shone his light on it and realized it was blood.

Everything in him went cold. The other man that had brought them here, the one he had shot. He had assumed the man had made it topside before the charges went off, but clearly he had passed this way after the ship had tilted on to its side which meant there was a very real chance he was still

297

trapped in here with them.

The possibility of death by something other than drowning reared its head and he ground his teeth. They didn't have time to be cautious and go slow. Worse, with his flashlight there was a very real possibility that the other man would see them coming and have the advantage. Jeremiah just hoped he was as worried about escaping the ship as they were and he wouldn't take the time to stop and ambush them.

He briefly debated sharing his information with Cindy, but decided against it. She had enough to worry about and no good would come out of giving her more stress at the moment. If they were lucky, she'd never have to know that they were trapped in the sinking ship with a killer.

He pressed forward, looking for more signs of blood. A wounded man could be twice as dangerous as a normal one. He wanted to know if they were still following his path or not. Hopefully he would know the way out and it meant they were going in the right direction.

He thought about the tracker he still had in his sock. He doubted it was water proof and it had probably failed already. But it should have been working up until the water hit them. So, why hadn't Kapono arrived with the cavalry yet? Why hadn't they rescued them while they were in the raft before they even made it to the boat.

He hoped the police had already captured the men on board the yacht. They shouldn't have been that far behind him and they should have realized when he was no longer on the yacht so they would have known it was safe to close in on the boat without risking a hostage standoff.

But why hadn't they come yet? Kapono had given him the tracker specifically so they could hone in on his location, under the assumption that he would find Cindy faster than the police. Hopefully the device itself had been functioning properly and not faulty.

Deep, groaning sounds reverberated through the ship. Behind him he could feel Cindy jump and her hand landed on his arm.

"What's that?" she cried.

"Metal giving way. The ship wasn't designed to be under water. Plus, the areas around the explosions have been weakened. It's twisting, tearing itself apart," he said.

There was silence behind him but her hand gripped his arm tighter.

"It's nothing we need to worry about at the moment," he said quickly. It was a lie.

Those were bad sounds and could mean a host of things that could make their situation worse very quickly. She didn't need to know that, though.

He pushed forward and they found another passageway with a ladder. On the wall he saw more blood. At the rate the man was bleeding, he was likely to bleed to death before making it out of the ship. The wound shouldn't have been fatal, but it would require pressure placed on it quickly to stop the bleeding which this guy obviously had not taken the time to do. They walked carefully by the ladder and then he stepped cautiously into another corridor.

Jeremiah twisted his head to the right, shining his penlight down the new corridor to see if he could see any more openings. There were none. He turned his head toward the left just in time to see a fist swinging at him.

He dropped and twisted and the fist grazed his temple. The man he had wounded stood over him, features twisted in rage.

Cindy saw Jeremiah drop and a hand flash by his head. She jumped back a step and forced down a scream. They weren't alone on the ship. It must be one of their other captors, she realized. And apparently the man still wanted them dead.

She looked around frantically, searching for something she could use to hit him with, but there was nothing. Jeremiah must have hit the man's legs because he toppled over backward and Jeremiah jumped on top of him. The two began flailing in the water, sometimes beneath it, sometimes on top of it.

She saw the penlight drift down to the ground, knocked free of Jeremiah's hand. With it a few feet below water everything was so much darker. Fear crept around her heart as she could no longer tell the combatants apart. Jeremiah was fighting for his life, for *their* lives, with a killer. There had to be something she could do to help.

But in order to help she had to be able to see better. Without giving herself more time to think about it she took a deep breath and then plunged under the water. She forced herself to open her eyes even though it stung and frightened her more. Just three feet away was the penlight and she reached down for it.

A flailing foot nearly kicked her in the head, but she twisted out of the way. She reached for the penlight, stretching her arm and her fingers as far as she could. Someone slammed into her and she grunted, expelling half her air. She was going to have to go up, but they were running out of time. If ever she was going to do this it had to be now.

She grabbed hold of the opening they had been stepping through, and pulled herself farther down. She was fighting the buoyancy of the seawater and her own crushing fear.

Her fingertips grazed the penlight and then she grasped it. She swung it up and shone it on the two fighters and pushed herself to the surface. She sucked in air with a gasp and tried to track what was happening in front of her. The other man had his back to Cindy but she could see that his hands were wrapped around Jeremiah's throat. He was wearing a black tank top and she could see an oozing hole in the back of his left shoulder. It looked almost like a bullet hole. Regardless of what it was, it was clearly a bad injury.

Cindy stepped closer so that she would be in range of the man. Then, she grasped the penlight as tightly as she could, lifted it over her head and then swung it down, straight into the wound on the back of the man's shoulder.

He let out a scream unlike anything she'd ever heard before and dropped Jeremiah instantly as he began to thrash around, reaching for his back. He knocked Cindy backward, but she managed to keep hold of her feet and the light.

Meanwhile Jeremiah had gone on the attack. "Do it again!" he shouted as the man turned his attention back to him.

Cindy hit the man again. Blood gushed from the wound, painting the water around her red. She hit him a third time. Her fear of the water was gone, everything else replaced by her need to stop the man from hurting Jeremiah.

The man's struggling became weaker. They were winning, she realized. She took a step back, waiting to see what Jeremiah wanted her to do.

Jeremiah shoved the man's head under water, drowning him, and she watched, heart racing. Then he hauled him up out of the water. The fight had gone out of the man, though, and she realized that he was dying.

"Which way?" Jeremiah demanded, leaning over him.

The man said something, but Cindy couldn't make it out. Then he was gone.

Jeremiah dropped his body back under the water.

"What did he say?" she asked.

Jeremiah pointed to the left. "He said it was this way."

But she noticed that he wouldn't meet her eyes and she had a sneaking suspicion that he was just guessing. She didn't say anything, though. She could be wrong.

Jeremiah headed to the left and Cindy followed, shivering when her leg brushed by the body. They slogged forward several more yards and the fear of the water began to overtake her again as they left the dead man farther behind.

"How much further?" Cindy asked.

"We need to get another deck toward the top, possibly two before we can get free of the ship."

"Are we going to make it?" she gasped, her teeth beginning to chatter as the water swirled above her waist.

"We're going to try," he said grimly, pushing on. "What killed that man?" she asked, fearfully.

"A bullet wound. He was bleeding out slowly. There was no way he would have made it much farther in the shape he was in."

"So, I . . . I didn't kill him?" she said, remembering the gush of blood.

"No, I did, when I shot him earlier. His brain just hadn't gotten the message yet," he said, his voice gruff.

She felt relief rush through her. And as her worry over that subsided her fear of dying there in the dark, underwater came rushing back.

She told herself that they had defeated their captors and they could defeat this, too.

It was getting harder to move, though, the water dragging at every step. It reminded her of when she had been a little kid and tried to run out of the pool. Her legs were burning with the effort of moving so quickly. But they didn't have the luxury of making their way more slowly. She followed right behind Jeremiah, trusting him to help them avoid sudden openings since she could no longer see the walls they were walking on through the dark water. His penlight was shining just a couple of feet ahead of her, a beacon of light.

Finally they found another passageway leading to a higher deck and were scrambling. The water was swirling ever higher and it was now at her chest. She kicked something with her foot and pain spiked up her leg.

Jeremiah twisted to look at her.

"I'm fine," she said. It was a lie. She was beyond exhausted and she wasn't sure how she was even standing upright. It had to be the adrenalin, she theorized, but how long did that stuff work before it wore off?

God. God had to be keeping her alive, keeping her moving. Maybe He still had a plan, a work for her to do. She had to keep going, keep trying, even if it felt like her legs were too heavy to take another step or her heart was racing so fast it felt like it was going to burst out of her chest. Truth was, she was so exhausted that she was even starting to fight to stay awake, to keep going. But every time she nearly stopped, the fear would kick in, prodding her, reminding her. To stop moving was to die.

"Do you need me to carry you?"

"No, just get us out of here."

Just get us out of here.

Cindy's words rang in Jeremiah's ears. She was placing so much faith and trust in him and she had no idea just how hopeless their situation actually was. His knowledge of these kinds of ships was so limited that he was little better than stumbling around in the dark.

He cast the penlight back and forth, keeping it going, trying to find the path they needed. He would have thought there would have been someplace on the ship where you could access all the desks, a central stair location. If there was, so far he hadn't found it. Of course, thanks to the water that was slowing them down more and more they probably weren't traveling as far as one would have thought.

He pushed forward, saying a prayer for safety, for strength. And he kept wondering where Kapono was. Why hadn't they been picked up before they had been brought onboard this ship?

It didn't sit right with him. He let his mind puzzle over it to combat the creeping fear that he was going to fail and that Cindy was going to die in the middle of the ocean and it would somehow be his fault.

A terrible suspicion dawned on him. What if Kapono was playing both sides? That would explain why no rescue had arrived. But if that were the case wouldn't he have simply handed over the bank account number on the card after he got it from Cindy?

Unless he was planning on ransoming the account information or he worked for a competitor. Dark thoughts swirled in Jeremiah's mind even as the water swirled around his waist. He ran back through in his mind everything Kapono had said and done since picking him up at the airport.

At least he knew for a fact that Mark had called someone on the Honolulu police force for help. But maybe Kapono had seized the opportunity to insinuate himself into the position of liaison. But for what purpose? Maybe he wanted to sell the account numbers to their owner but he didn't actually know who they belonged to so he needed to discover the identity of the man behind Cindy's kidnapping first.

It made a terrible kind of sense. If it was true there was no help coming, not even when they made it to the surface. Jeremiah had woken up in the raft and had no idea how long they had been out to sea, how many miles from shore they were.

One thing at a time, he cautioned himself. He didn't need to figure out how they were going to swim back to shore or find a boat to pick them up. All he had to figure out now was how to get out of the ship. Then they had to swim to the surface. There were a lot of steps that had to be accomplished successfully before he could even begin to worry about being adrift. And step one wasn't going well.

The only thing going in their favor was how slowly the ship was sinking. If they did make it out they were going to need a fighting chance of getting to the surface with just the oxygen in their lungs. From what he could tell anything remotely useful on board the ship had already been stripped out. They were on their own.

The ship began to tilt slightly, back toward being right side up. It wasn't much but it was disconcerting, and if it kept going the ladders could become a real issue.

The water rose, swirling around his chest and just under Cindy's chin. They were running out of time. And then he saw a murky light shining in front of them. He pushed forward as fast as he could until he could make out portholes in the ship submerged under the water.

He stopped and Cindy looked down. He took a deep breath and then dove under the water. The latch on the window still worked, but there was too much water pressure on either side to allow it to swing open. His only chance was to break the glass which was already under a terrific strain.

He pulled the gun out of his pocket. He wished it was a Glock 17 which was designed so it could be fired underwater. What he had, though, was a Sig Sauer P239 which meant he'd be able to fire it, but only once. He was going to have to make the shot count.

He positioned the gun about six inches away from the glass and pulled the trigger. The bullet exploded outward, punching through the glass, shattering it. The casing didn't eject, jammed into the slide. He had expected that. He took the gun and smashed the lingering bits of glass clear from the porthole frame. He looked at it closely. The opening was two feet wide. It was wide enough for Cindy to get through, but not him.

He surfaced and Cindy gave a cry of relief. He looked at her. She was pale and shaking and there was terror in her eyes. The water was even higher now and she was struggling to keep her head above water.

"You're going to go down, out the port-hole, and then swim clear of the ship and up to the surface. You'll have to be careful to get out from under it. We should have you going out the top side, but I'm not sure we can cross over to it in time," he said.

"I'll follow you," she said resolutely.

He shook his head. "I could never get my shoulders through, it's too narrow. But you could make it."

"Not without you."

He picked her up so that her head was higher above water. It was rising much faster now. She put his arms around his neck and hung on, eyes pleading with him.

Cindy couldn't believe what Jeremiah was

saying to her. He couldn't be serious. How did he think she could go and leave him behind? After all that they had been through together, all that they had survived. They had to both make it out of here alive. Anything else was insanity and she wouldn't hear it.

"It's the only way," Jeremiah said with a gasp.

"No! I can't leave you. We'll make it, there has to be a way. We'll keep walking, we have to find our way out. I won't leave."

"You have to," he insisted, struggling to get the words out around the water that was beginning to rush into his mouth. "I'll keep trying to go up. But this is the best . . . chance."

She took a last breath of air before the water rose above her lips and shook her head wildly. She didn't want to leave him. How could she after all this?

And in her mind she saw her sister, dead, eyes frozen open. And the image morphed instead into Jeremiah. She hit his chest with her fists and pointed onward, but he shook his head.

Then he grabbed her around the waist and twisted her around. She struggled, but he was too strong. Then he was shoving her out the porthole, pushing until her legs were clear.

As soon as she was out she spun around, staring at him through the porthole. He gave her a small, sad smile and then sank from her sight.

18

Cindy wanted to scream, but her lungs were already burning for air. She stared into the porthole, but it had grown too dark and she couldn't see anything.

Her lungs ached harder and her legs began to kick almost involuntarily. She bumped her head against the side of the ship and then shook it to clear her vision. Then she turned and saw pale light above her. She kicked for all she was worth and got free of the ship and then she began clawing upward with arms too. She began to blow tiny bubbles out of her mouth, desperate to expel the carbon dioxide that was building up.

She was getting weaker. Her body had already been wracked by exhaustion and deprivation. She realized she couldn't make it much longer. The surface seemed so far away. She flailed wildly. She started to lose her vision.

And then, just as her lungs felt like they were going to burst, she broke the surface. She gulped in a huge lungful of air and then let it out in one terrible scream.

The sun was rising on the horizon. A new day was dawning. A day without Jeremiah. She screamed again, hearing the sound as though it were being ripped out of her body. She thrashed in the water, panicking, as her mind began to process where she was and not just what had happened.

She was treading water in the ocean. She twisted her head around, looking for the land. She finally saw it, but it was so far away it might as well have not been there at all.

Jeremiah's dead and I will be, too.

Several yards away from her there was a disturbance in the water and then a fin broke the surface. She stared in consternation. Just when things couldn't possibly get worse they always seemed to.

What was she supposed to do to survive a shark attack? All she could think about were admonitions she had heard on the news not to 'look like a seal'. Well, she had no idea if she looked like a seal, but she did know that she was wearing the black dress still, and that it was mushrooming around her in the water.

This can't be happening.

Punch them in the nose. She had heard that someone did that and lived. But that meant the shark had to be really close, and you had to be swinging towards all those teeth. And she could barely keep herself at the surface of the water.

She should flip onto her back, float for a while and save her energy, but then she couldn't watch the fin that was slowly circling. Was it getting closer or was she imagining it?

No, it definitely was getting closer, and now it was turning toward her. She screamed again, and prepared to hit at whatever came at her. But how could she know how big it was, how far the nose was from the fin? She tried to see if she could see a shadow moving in the water, but with the way the sun was angled, she couldn't.

"Please, God, save me!" she screamed her prayer to the heavens.

And then the fin shot upward and the entire creature leaped out of the water and then slammed back down into it a moment later.

A dolphin. It was a dolphin and not a shark.

She was sobbing and shaking and she was aware that her legs were slowing down. She needed to flip onto her back, had to.

A roaring sound filled her ears and slowly she became aware of it. It seemed to be coming from behind her. Then she heard a shout. She turned her head and saw a boat headed her way with someone waving frantically. She didn't have the strength to lift her arm to wave. She wasn't even sure if she had the strength to keep treading water until they reached her.

The boat slowed as it moved closer and frustration filled her. They needed to go faster, not slower. She couldn't hold on any longer. Then she saw Kapono, standing on the edge of the boat.

He dove into the water, and swam to her, and grabbed her around the chest, holding her up as the boat maneuvered closer. Then he swam the couple remaining feet, dragging her with him and there were many hands that lifted her out of the water and laid her down on the deck.

"Where's Jeremiah?" Kapono asked.

The only answer she could give was another scream.

Someone was beside her checking her over. "It's okay," he was murmuring over and over again. She registered that he seemed to be some sort of medic. How could she tell him that nothing would ever be okay again?

She didn't know how they had found her, and she was grateful that they had, but it felt like her soul was lying with Jeremiah in a watery grave far below.

"She's in shock," she heard the medic tell someone.

"Of course she is," she heard Kapono answer.

The boat rocked up and down. She felt like she was going to be sick. "I want to sit up," she finally said.

"You'd be better off laying down," the medic said.

She shook her head and he slowly helped her to a sitting position. Her head was spinning and she wanted to curl into a ball and sleep. She didn't want to throw up, though. Of course, what could there possibly be in her system to expel?

"Water," she said.

Someone handed her a bottle of water but her hand was shaking too hard to hold it. Then Kapono knelt down next to her and held it for her, tipping it slowly into her mouth. The first attempt left her sputtering and choking, but the second attempt she got some of it down. She nodded when she was done.

"How did you find me?" she asked.

"Jeremiah . . . he had a tracker on him. Then, we heard you screaming while we were searching for you. Can you tell me what happened?" Kapono asked after he had put the water away.

She shuddered and closed her eyes. She was going to have to talk about it and she knew that the sooner she did, the more likely they could catch the people who were responsible.

"The owner of the yacht, *Pearl of the Deep,* is behind everything. He called himself Mr. Black, but I don't think that's his real name."

"That's okay, we caught him," Kapono assured her. "He's in jail downtown as we speak and he won't be getting out for a long, long time."

She shuddered, grateful, at least, for that much.

"Man overboard!"

She jerked as she heard someone shouting. Everyone scrambled to the side of the boat, looking out at the ocean. *Had someone fallen in?* she wondered. That seemed strange. Whatever was going on, though, everyone seemed to be getting more and more agitated.

She twisted her head to see what was going on.

They were lifting someone into the boat. Then they set him down and she craned her neck to see who it was.

Someone moved out of the way and her heart stopped and then restarted.

It was Jeremiah.

Jeremiah sat gasping on the bottom of the boat, relieved to see that Cindy was already there. He had been so worried that she wouldn't make it. He gave her a smile and she just stared at him like she'd seen a ghost. Then she seemed to come alive and she crawled over to him and threw her arms around him.

He held her close and thanked G-d that they were both alive. It was a miracle, nothing less.

"You escaped?" she asked wonderingly.

"I found the next passageway about thirty feet from the porthole. There were still a few pockets of air in there and then I found the one that led me out." It had been a little more complicated than that, but there was no reason to share the details. It was enough that they were both alive.

Finally she pulled away and Kapono handed him a bottle of water. He took it gratefully, but glared at the big detective.

"What kept you?" Jeremiah asked Kapono.

The detective grimaced. "The navy. By the time we figured out where you were they were about to blow the ship and they wouldn't let us get any closer. In the minute it took me to explain the situation to them the explosives had already gone off. We assumed the worst."

Jeremiah nodded. "I was beginning to think I had misjudged you."

"Nah. I got your back, bruddah."

"Good to know," Jeremiah said as he drank down the bottle of water.

He turned to say something to Cindy but she was curled up on the floor next to him asleep. He touched her cheek briefly then turned back to Kapono.

"She should see a doctor."

He nodded. "Our medic was checking her out." He turned and indicated another man.

"Apart from the obvious dehydration and exhaustion she's got some nasty cuts, but she should be okay."

Jeremiah nodded, grateful to hear that.

"The guy behind all this?"

"Caught him at his yacht along with several of his gang. We also found Manny in that alley and arrested him."

"Figured you would," Jeremiah said.

"You gave me quite a scare."

Jeremiah nodded. "I'll take another water."

Once they made it back to shore they transported Cindy and Jeremiah to the hospital. After being checked out he was released right away, but they admitted Cindy and immediately set her up on IV drips to help her body regain the fluids it had lost. Her cuts were cleaned and she was also given a boatload of antibiotics just to be on the safe side.

Later that afternoon he was sitting in her room when she woke up.

"Hey, how are you doing?" he asked.

"Hungry," she admitted.

"That's a good sign."

"I thought you were dead," she said, staring at him with large, moist eyes.

"I was a bit worried about that myself," he admitted. He wanted to downplay it, but realized he couldn't and that he probably shouldn't. She'd had every right to be that afraid.

"Thanks for rescuing me," she said.

"You're welcome."

She fell silent and he could see that she was still struggling with everything that had happened to her. He stood after a moment and she looked at him with panic in her eyes.

"There are some other people who wanted to say hello. I'm going to go tell them you're awake and I'll be right back. Okay?"

She nodded.

It felt like Jeremiah was gone for an eternity although she knew it could only really be a couple of minutes. When he returned Kapono, and Charles and Jean, the couple from the luau, were with him. They all took turns hugging her.

"We owe you both a debt of gratitude," Kapono said. "You've solved more cases in the last few days than some people solve in a lifetime."

"Don't take this the wrong way," she said, "but I can't really say I was glad to help."

He smiled. "Not taken the wrong way at all. I'm sure the two of you just want to go home, but the city would be happy to put you up for a few days, give you a proper vacation."

She shook her head. "Maybe some other time."

"Of course. Well, the good news is I just talked to the doctor and he'll clear you to go home tomorrow as long as everything goes well tonight."

She nodded, grateful for that bit of news. She wanted to be home in her own bed, and put the entire nightmare behind her. "So, no worry about anything, okay?"

"Okay," she said.

"We were very sorry to hear what happened to you," Jean said, when Kapono sat down in a chair. "If there's anything we can do, just let us know."

"Thanks."

"No, thank you for uncovering what was happening on the north shore," Charles said. "The archaeology firm I work for is headquartered on this island and they've been tasked with straightening the whole mess out. Just from the work that's been done this morning they can already determine that the bodies are from multiple time periods and they're working to figure out which parts of the island they all came from. I'd say the entire island owes you a debt of gratitude."

"Not to mention that resort which will most likely be able to continue building," Jean noted.

"So, they were digging up the bodies from other areas?" Cindy said. "I was wondering about that."

"You were right," Jeremiah jumped in. "I questioned Al as one of the suspects in your disappearance and he was able to confirm it."

"So, he was trying to kill me with that life preserver, I wasn't just being paranoid?"

Cindy asked.

"Not even a little bit paranoid," Jeremiah confirmed. "He was worried you had uncovered the fact that they were burying bodies from other parts of the island there to halt the building of the resort. They were desecrating graves in the process and because of you everyone associated with that is now in jail."

"You're an all around hero," Kapono said.

She forced a smile. It was good that she had been able to help these people, but being a hero wasn't always all it was cracked up to be. "I just wanted to go on vacation," she said.

The others smiled, clearly not sure exactly what to say to her. That's okay, she wasn't sure what they could say that would make everything that had happened better.

Finally Charles and Jean left and Kapono and Jeremiah alone remained.

"There's one thing I don't understand," she said.

"What?" Jeremiah asked.

"Why go to all the trouble of trying to sink us on that ship instead of just killing us and dumping our bodies somewhere?"

"I can answer that one," Kapono said. "They knew the navy was planning on reefing one of their old ships to create an artificial reef for fish and divers. By leaving you alive to drown in the ship when your bodies were discovered it would look like you were just a couple of tourists who decided to go exploring somewhere they shouldn't of and got killed. It could be passed off as some kind of crazy accident. That's why they didn't just kill you. Plus, who knows, maybe they were hoping you'd make some sort of last minute bargain to try and save your lives. It's kind of ironic. All your troubles on the island started when you visited Pearl Harbor and the boat they were reefing was constructed around the same time as the Arizona."

Cindy thought of how Jeremiah had pushed her out of a portal, saving her life, and knew that irony didn't even begin to describe it.

In the morning she was feeling a bit better and the doctor agreed to release her. When she was shown the clothes she'd been admitted in, though, she was sickened.

Cindy looked down at the tattered remains of Geanie's little black dress. And for some reason that just made everything worse. Somehow it seemed symbolic of everything that had gone so terribly wrong.

"Clearly you can't wear that on the plane,"

Jeremiah said.

She jumped. She didn't realize he had entered the room. "No, I guess not."

"I packed up your things from the hotel and I brought you these to wear," he said, handing her her blue shirt and a pair of shorts. He also had her tennis shoes and socks. She realized that she had no idea what had even become of her sandals.

"Thank you."

The next couple of hours seemed to drag by as she got dressed and waited for the final orders from the hospital authorizing her release. It was more waiting and she was sick of it beyond belief.

Kapono showed up to drive them to the airport where there was still more waiting. Finally it was time to board.

Cindy didn't know how, but they ended up in first class on the flight home. She had to admit that the seats were so much comfier, but after what she'd been through she was sure even the regular seats would feel wonderful. She fell asleep before they even took off.

Jeremiah woke her when it was time to eat for which she was grateful. The food was much better in first class, though again she wasn't sure how much of that was her current perceptions.

Once she had finished eating she fell asleep again and didn't wake until they had actually made it to their gate at LAX. Jeremiah carried her small bag for her as they exited the plane. She was still a bit shaky when she walked, but she'd been assured that that would go away in a day or two. She began to think that she'd been foolish to refuse the wheelchair she'd been offered, though.

Still, how was life going to get back to normal if she didn't force the issue? So, she walked, wobbling occasionally, but resolutely putting one foot in front of the other as they headed to baggage claim. When they had almost reached it she realized that she didn't even actually know what day it was. Regardless, there was no way she was going back to work in the morning. Normalcy was a great thing, but she wasn't ready to deal with that quite yet.

When they got to baggage claim she felt herself tear up as she saw Mark, Traci, and Geanie standing there waiting for them. She ran over to Geanie and they hugged tight. "I'm sorry I ruined your dress!" she burst out, not knowing what else to say.

Geanie hugged her tighter. "I don't care about a stupid dress. I just thank God that you're home."

"Causing trouble in other people's jurisdictions, I'm not sure how I feel about that," Mark said, with a forced smile. She could see the worry in his eyes, though, and feel the sympathy coming off of him. She gave him a quick hug. Jeremiah had told her what the detective had done for her.

Next she hugged Traci and she could feel the sympathy coming off of her in waves. "I know what it's like. Thanks to you, what I went through wasn't nearly as terrible, but if you need to talk, I can at least understand," the other woman whispered.

"Thank you," Cindy whispered back.

19

Cindy woke up and it took a minute to orient herself. She finally realized she was back at home in her room. She sat up slowly, sore and so very tired. She showered and got dressed and headed out to the kitchen.

Geanie was busy bustling around. She looked up at her with bright eyes. "Morning. I thought you'd like some pancakes."

"Thank you," Cindy said, moving to the refrigerator to grab herself some orange juice. Then she sat down at the table which Geanie had already set.

"And, don't worry, I made plenty."

Cindy winced. "I guess I went a little crazy when I got home last night."

"I've never seen you eat that much food in a day let alone at one sitting," Geanie said.

"I guess it takes on a whole different meaning when you suddenly have a fear that you won't get enough, or that someone's going to starve you."

"I can't even imagine," Geanie said.

"I pray you never have to." Cindy took a sip of her orange juice and set it down. "I'm sorry. I didn't get a chance to scope out any hotels as good wedding locations."

Geanie stared at her like she'd grown a second head and then burst into crazy, cackling laughter. She walked over and wrapped her arms around Cindy hugging her tight.

"I can't even believe you're still thinking about that after everything that's happened."

"Well, I told you I'd look."

Geanie hugged her tighter. "Don't even worry about it. Besides, now that I think about it, who wants to do a small ceremony that no one can come to when we can do a large ceremony and have everyone come?"

Cindy felt a bit justified. She had never exactly pictured Geanie as the small ceremony type, even before she and Joseph got engaged.

"So, that means a wedding around here somewhere."

"Yes. I think January would be perfect, don't you?"

Cindy wrinkled her nose. It was so Geanie to go against the flow that way. "There's a good chance it will rain."

Geanie pulled away and the smile on her face was priceless. "It's good luck when it rains on your wedding day."

Geanie bounded back into the kitchen and returned seconds later with a heaping platter of pancakes which she set down with a flourish. Cindy grabbed a forkful and deposited them on her plate then reached for the syrup.

Geanie said a quick grace, including a thank you for Cindy's safe return. As soon as it was over Cindy brought a forkful of pancake to her lips.

"I actually have something I wanted to ask you, and, well, I know it's terrible timing."

Cindy raised an eyebrow and chomped down on her food while she waited for Geanie to ask whatever it was. The other woman looked suddenly awkward and shy and it seemed so ridiculous. After everything that had happened in the past week Cindy couldn't imagine what question was that difficult to ask her.

"I was wondering if you would be my maid of honor? I mean, without you Joseph and I would never have gotten together."

Even though they'd been talking about the wedding, somehow that was the last question Cindy had been expecting. She hastily swallowed the food in her mouth. "Yes, of course!" she said, struggling to sound happy. She was honored to be asked and under different circumstances she would have been thrilled. It was just hard to imagine at that moment that she was ever going to be happy again.

It's going to take time, that's all, she told herself. She leaned forward and gave Geanie a quick hug. "Thank you so much for asking me!"

Geanie squealed and clapped her hands. "We're going to have so much fun!"

Cindy felt a wave of sorrow crash around her. At that moment she'd give anything to be able to have fun. In that moment she realized just how much she had lost out on over the years, first with the way she shut down after what happened to her sister and now the kidnapping. Who knew how long before she would laugh and smile again?

"That sounds great," she said, sincerely.

As though sensing her mood, Geanie reached out and grabbed her hand. "I don't know how to be around you," she said, suddenly.

Tears welled in Cindy's eyes. "They say with things like Post Traumatic Stress Disorder the most important thing is to just have people around who care about you, who are patient."

Geanie sighed. "I care about you, but no one on this earth would call me patient."

"That's true."

"But I'll do my best."

"So will I," Cindy promised. "Hopefully in a couple of weeks I'll be just fine."

"I'm praying for a couple of days. Told you. Not patient."

Cindy hugged her again and then went back to her pancakes.

"Oh, I should warn you," Geanie said. "They're throwing you a welcome home party at church tomorrow."

"Is it wrong that I kind of don't want to go?"

"No."

"But I guess it's just as much for everyone else as it is for me."

"We were all terrified," Geanie said. "We were holding prayer vigils around the clock in the sanctuary once Detective Walters called and told me you'd been kidnapped."

"I appreciate it," Cindy said, tears stinging her eyes again.

"I just wanted you to know ahead of time. Although, I did warn them not to all jump out and shout surprise or anything like that."

"Thank you," Cindy said gratefully.

Geanie shrugged. "We'll see. I'm not sure if anybody listened."

Mark was sitting in the Dryer family living room, being stared down by Denise Dryer, the matriarch, and the mother of the real Paul Dryer. Sitting next to her was her daughter, Gretchen, and across the room was Paul's father, Bryce. The man was letting his wife do all the talking and Mark couldn't help but feel like he was losing the battle, his one real shot at talking to the Dryer family about their son and his changeling.

"A police officer did inform us of the unfortunate . . . mix up with the DNA analysis for the body of a child they discovered. I want to reassure you, Mr. Walters, that whoever that was, it was not our son. Our son was a police detective and he died a hero just a few weeks ago. Whoever that other child was I wish they would figure it out so that his mother can have her mind put to rest, but trust me, it was not our boy."

Denise Dryer had a southern accent, the only one in her family that did, and she was one of the only people in Pine Springs who sported an accent from the other side of the country. She had an imperiousness to her that said that she had always had money. She knew how to command a room.

Mark cleared his throat. He had worked hard to get this interview. He shouldn't even be there, harassing the family. He was sure the only reason he had made it through the front door was that he had been Paul's partner. Rather, he had been Not Paul's partner, but he could sense that he wasn't going to convince Denise of that.

On some level he guessed she had the right to believe what she wanted. He, however, had an obligation to the truth, and to both Pauls to find out what had really happened to each of them and who Not Paul really was.

"I understand that this is difficult, but perhaps if you can just humor me for a moment on this, I have a few questions."

"I'm sorry, Mr. Walters, but you're five minutes are up. I let you in to this house because you were a friend to my boy. But we're done here and you can leave now," Denise Dryer said as she rose gracefully to her feet.

He stood slowly, struggling not to let his impatience and his frustration show. The last thing he needed was for her to report his visit, especially since he wasn't there in any official capacity.

335

He pulled a business card out of his pocket and put it down on the coffee table. "Thank you for your time. If anyone has anything to say," he said, sweeping the room with his eyes, "I can be reached at this number."

The older woman didn't even acknowledge that he had spoken, just stared fixedly at the space above his head. He set his jaw and turned to go. "I'll see myself out."

As he passed through the massive marble foyer he couldn't help but think about Joseph, the parishioner from First Shepherd he'd had the occasion to run into now several times. He had to move in the same circles as the Dryers, but you'd never guess it from his attitude.

Joseph was a few years Paul's junior, so they wouldn't have probably known each other growing up. It was worth asking, though. If nothing else maybe Joseph knew something about the family that could help. Sometimes gossip provided just the right lead that would otherwise go undiscovered.

He was down the long walkway and halfway to his car when he heard running steps behind him.

"Wait!"

Mark turned around and saw Gretchen running toward him. He stopped and she reached him in a moment and put a hand on his arm. "Did you mean it? Paul's really not my, wasn't, I mean, my brother?"

Her eyes were soft and pleading and it killed him to nod his head.

"I'm afraid he wasn't," he said, trying to say it as gently as he could even though he knew that would do nothing to ease the pain of her loss or her sense of confusion and betrayal that must surely follow.

She nodded her head slowly and bit her lip.

"You knew that already, didn't you?" he asked with a flash of insight.

"I-I don't want to talk about it."

"Gretchen, you have to tell me what you know. I mean, who knows? Maybe he had family, a real sister out there somewhere who never knew what happened to him, just like you never knew what happened to your real brother."

Tears filled her eyes. "You have to understand. Paul, whoever he was, I'll always love him, think of him as if he were really my brother."

"That's understandable," Mark said, sensing that she was wavering, at a crossroads. He needed her to choose a path and he needed it to be the one that gave him information. "But he was a detective, unsolved crimes drove him crazy. Someone killed your real brother and for some reason the man we knew as Paul took his place. For all we know he didn't even realize that he wasn't your brother. We owe it to both of them to find out what happened."

She took a deep breath. "You're right, I guess. I do owe them both."

"Yes. So, please, tell me what you know."

"When we were little Paul was kidnapped by our nanny. I was five. He was eight. The police searched everywhere but eventually they gave up. Almost two years later we got a call. Police had picked him up wandering on the side of a road. He was injured and he had these terrible scars on his face and a broken nose. But he knew who he was, his address and phone number and the police brought him home. He said that the nanny had been holding him in a cabin by a lake, but she was never found."

Gretchen dropped her eyes to the ground. "My parents were overjoyed. A few weeks later they had a plastic surgeon fix his face up. Paul was so happy to be home and he knew everything about everyone, the house. No one even questioned that it might not be him."

"Except for you."

"Except for me. He looked similar and

338

two years and all those scars and who could tell if he really was the same kid. We had a fort in a tree in the backyard that was our special place. Three days after he came home he came out to the fort where I was and he didn't know our secret password to get in."

Mark frowned. It wasn't the game changing piece of information he was hoping for. "It had been almost two years and as you pointed out there was so much trauma."

"There was no way he would have forgotten," she insisted, crossing her arms. "He remembered all kinds of stupid things, like what presents I got at my birthday party the month before he was kidnapped. But he didn't know the one secret that we had. Not only did he not know the password, but he also didn't even know there was a password. Even weirder when I finally told him what it was it seemed to freak him out."

"The word itself freaked him out?"

"Yes."

"What did you do?" Mark prompted.

"I told Mom and Dad."

"But they didn't believe you," Mark guessed.

"No. They told me what you did just now. And when I insisted they thought that I was just jealous because he was getting so much attention."

The tears that she had been holding back began to roll down her cheeks. "It was terrible, unfair. They didn't get that I wanted him to be home as much as they did."

"Thank you for telling me that," Mark said.

She nodded.

"Was there anything else unusual, different about him?"

"He used to be a fussy eater when we were little, but after he came back he ate everything. We always thought it was because he was just grateful to be home and to have enough food. He was super skinny when he came home. And he didn't want to ever go to church again. He said he spent two years praying that someone would rescue him and no one ever did. Mom and Dad made him go but after a few weeks they just let him stay home."

He turned and walked the few remaining feet to his car. "Before I go can you just answer one more question?"

"I'll try."

"What was your secret password?"

She smiled. "We picked it one day after Sunday School because of the way the teacher kept using the word. She had this really funny accent and it made us laugh.

Our password was *Righteousness.*"

Jeremiah returned to the house after running some errands. He was wired, keyed up still. And there were still so many questions about the future that he wasn't ready to face. Captain was overjoyed to have him home and he took the dog for a short walk. They had just made it back to the house when his phone rang.

"Hi, Mark," Jeremiah said. "Thanks again for everything," he said.

"I wish I could have done more," the detective said. "I'm so very sorry."

"Thank you."

The detective cleared his throat. "I'm sorry to call, but I wanted to let you know that I found out some more information about what it was like when Not Paul was found as a kid. The sister opened up and talked to me."

"That's great. Speaking of Not Paul, we should get back to our sessions."

Mark hesitated. "I didn't want to push you."

"It's important. I need to regain some normalcy and you need to keep progressing so you can get cleared to work again."

There was another hesitation and then Mark asked quietly, "Do you think that will ever happen again?"

Jeremiah rubbed his eyes with his free hand. Mark was in a bad place and he needed reassurance. As a counselor, that wasn't Jeremiah's place. It was his place to listen and evaluate. As a friend, though, he owed him something more.

He cleared his throat. "You asked me once if I thought you did the right thing."

"Yes?" Mark asked, and from the tone of his voice Jeremiah could tell the other man wasn't sure if he wanted to hear the answer.

"I think you did."

The relief in Mark's voice was painfully apparent. "So, in my shoes you would have done the same thing?"

Jeremiah took a deep breath. "No, in your shoes, I would have killed him."

There was silence for a long time and then Mark finally said, "Thank you."

"You're welcome," Jeremiah said. "I'll see you Thursday." He hung up before the detective could say anything.

He made a mental note to tell Marie to put it on his schedule. He had called her briefly the night before and learned that the only thing he had really missed when he had been gone had been an ant infestation. Otto, it seemed, had never shown up for his Wednesday appointment and neither of them knew even his last name or contact info. Jeremiah wasn't sure what had happened to change the old man's mind about keeping the appointment, but when Otto decided to talk, maybe he'd pop up again. Until then, he had far more pressing things to take care of.

After breakfast Cindy didn't know what to do with herself. She'd already talked to her parents the night before and even her brother, Kyle. She'd been so grateful to be alive and to hear their voices that she hadn't even thrown any darts at the dartboard that had Kyle's face on it on the back of her door. She had kept up the practice although since having to throw darts at actual people on St. Patrick's Day it seemed much more gruesome than it used to. Now, though, she was determined not to let the skill go rusty, just in case.

As soon as the breakfast dishes had been cleared away Geanie had gone into full wedding preparation mode. She and Joseph were going out to look at a few places where they might be able to hold a reception. They invited her along, but Cindy wasn't in the mood.

Once she was home alone, though, she realized that the last thing she wanted was to be alone. It just reminded her of slowly starving alone in the house her captors had stuck her in. By the time it was noon she was climbing the walls.

She finally drove over to Jeremiah's house. She wanted to see how he was. When she got there she realized he might actually be at the synagogue but to her relief he opened his door.

"How are you?" he asked as he stepped back to let her in.

She opened her mouth and words escaped her. He was watching her so intently as he closed the door. She threw her arms around him and buried her face in his chest and began to sob. She felt him wrap his arms around her and hold her. At one point she could tell he was rubbing her back. Later he was stroking her hair. And through it all he kept speaking, whisper soft. As the tears began to dry, she realized he was speaking in Hebrew, and a minute later realized that he must have been praying the entire time.

"I'm sorry," she whispered at last as she pulled away. She stared at the wet spot her tears had left on his pale blue shirt.

"There is nothing to be sorry about," he told her. "Do you believe me?"

She nodded her head.

"Good. Now come in and let's sit down.

Can I get you anything to drink?"

"Soda, if you have it."

A minute later they were seated on the couch in the living room. He had set two sodas and an envelope down on the coffee table.

"I thought you might be at the synagogue this morning."

He shrugged. "Marie had already lined up a replacement and I took advantage of it. Besides, I have a sneaking suspicion they're planning some kind of surprise. I figured I could wait a week to find out what it is."

"I'm getting a party tomorrow at church Geanie tells me."

"You're friends want to celebrate your safe return."

She wrapped her arms around herself. "I just don't feel like celebrating."

"I understand. You've been through a great shock. It will take a while for things to return to normal."

"Will they ever?" she asked him, staring deeply into his eyes.

He had a past. She was sure of that now. Things that he hid from her, from the world. Something told her that he could help her with what she was going through.

He shrugged. "They might. Then again, they might not."

"What do I do if they don't?"

"You learn to adapt, survive. Life will change, but that is not all bad. And one day you will wake up and realize that you are no longer as afraid as you were."

"I've spent my whole life afraid and I'm tired of it."

He gave her a tight smile. "Acknowledging that is the first step in fighting back."

She buried her face in her hands. "I don't want to be afraid anymore."

"Then don't be."

It seemed so simple when he said it that way, but how did one overcome a lifetime of fear?

"I mean, this is ridiculous," she said, looking up at him. "I want to feel good, happy, alive."

"You will," he promised.

"I don't want to be terrified of going on vacation again, of what will happen."

"You know, there's a simple solution, really to that one," he said, and something in his voice sounded different, excited, eager maybe.

"And what's that?" Cindy asked.

"You can't go on vacation by yourself anymore."

She stared at him, waiting for him to crack a smile, but he didn't.

346

"What did you have in mind?" she questioned, somewhat bewildered.

"I'm glad you asked," he said, grinning. "Seeing as how you've been really needing a vacation and you didn't get one, I thought something like this might be in order." He slid the envelope across the coffee table to her.

She picked it up and opened it, curiosity burning inside her. When she pulled out the contents she couldn't help but stare for a moment. Then, slowly, she felt a grin begin to spread across her face.

"So, Cindy, what are we going to do next?" he asked, a twinkle in his eye.

She waved the tickets in the air. "We're going to Disneyland!"

ABOUT THE AUTHOR

Debbie Viguié is the *New York Times* bestselling author of two dozen novels including the Wicked series, the Crusade series and the Wolf Springs Chronicles series co-authored with Nancy Holder. Debbie also writes thrillers including The Psalm 23 Mysteries, the Kiss trilogy, and the Witch Hunt trilogy. When Debbie isn't busy writing she enjoys spending time with her husband, Scott, visiting theme parks. They live in Florida with their cat, Schrödinger.